"You should marry, Professor." She added, "Someone suitable, of course."

"How unpleasant that sounds! You consider that I have reached an age when a suitable marriage is all that is left for me?"

"Heavens, no. I'm not sure exactly how old you are, but William said thirty-five—that's not in the least old—just right, in fact."

"But I do not wish to make a suitable marriage, Miss Partridge—a tepid love and a well-ordered life with ups and downs. I would wish for fun, a few healthy quarrels and a love to toss me to the skies."

He turned to look at her, smiling, so she knew that his words weren't meant to be taken seriously.

"Would you consider yourself to be a suitable wife for me, little Partridge?"

I¹1011756

Romance readers around the world were sad to note the passing of **Betty Neels** in June 2001. Her career spanned thirty years, and she continued to write into her ninetieth year. To her millions of fans, Betty epitomized the romance writer, and yet she began writing almost by accident. She had retired from nursing, but her inquiring mind still sought stimulation. Her new career was born when she heard a lady in her local library bemoaning the lack of good romance novels. Betty's first book, *Sister Peters in Amsterdam*, was published in 1969, and she eventually completed 134 books. Her novels offer a reassuring warmth that was very much a part of her own personality. She was a wonderful writer, and she will be greatly missed. Her spirit and genuine talent will live on in all her stories.

THE BEST *of*

BETTY NEELS

A STAR LOOKS DOWN

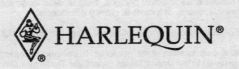

TORONTO • NEW YORK • LONDON
AMSTERDAM • PARIS • SYDNEY • HAMBURG
STOCKHOLM • ATHENS • TOKYO • MILAN • MADRID
PRAGUE • WARSAW • BUDAPEST • AUCKLAND

If you purchased this book without a cover you should be aware that this book is stolen property. It was reported as "unsold and destroyed" to the publisher, and neither the author nor the publisher has received any payment for this "stripped book."

ISBN-13: 978-0-373-19884-9
ISBN-10:   0-373-19884-1

A STAR LOOKS DOWN

Copyright © 1975 by Betty Neels.

All rights reserved. Except for use in any review, the reproduction or utilization of this work in whole or in part in any form by any electronic, mechanical or other means, now known or hereafter invented, including xerography, photocopying and recording, or in any information storage or retrieval system, is forbidden without the written permission of the publisher, Harlequin Enterprises Limited, 225 Duncan Mill Road, Don Mills, Ontario, Canada M3B 3K9.

This is a work of fiction. Names, characters, places and incidents are either the product of the author's imagination or are used fictitiously, and any resemblance to actual persons, living or dead, business establishments, events or locales is entirely coincidental.

This edition published by arrangement with Harlequin Books S.A.

® and TM are trademarks of the publisher. Trademarks indicated with ® are registered in the United States Patent and Trademark Office, the Canadian Trade Marks Office and in other countries.

www.eHarlequin.com

Printed in U.S.A.

CHAPTER ONE

IT was going to be a lovely day, but Beth Partridge, tearing round the little kitchen, hadn't had time to do more than take a cursory look out of the window; on duty at eight o'clock meant leaving the flat at seven-thirty sharp, and that entailed getting up at half past six—and every minute of that hour filled.

She worked tidily as well as fast; the flat looked pristine as she closed its front door and tore down the three flights of stairs, ran smartly out of the entrance and round the corner to the shed where she kept her bike. A minute later she was weaving her way in and out of London's early morning traffic, a slim figure with long legs, her titian hair, arranged in a great bun above her neck, glowing above the blue sweater and slacks. It took her exactly twenty minutes this morning; ten minutes, she thought with satisfaction, in which to change into uniform and take a quick look round the Recovery Room to make sure that everything was just as she had left it the evening before. She rounded one of the brick pillars, which marked the entrance to St Elmer's Hospital, going much too fast and before she could stop herself, ran into a man; fortunately a large man, who withstood the shock of a bicycle wheel in his back with considerable aplomb, putting out an unhurried hand to steady her handlebars and bring her to a halt before he turned round.

She had put out a leg to steady herself, and now, the bike slightly askew, she stood astride it, returning his calm, unhurried examination of her person with what dignity she could muster. He had a nice face; a little rugged perhaps, but good-looking, although the nose was too beaky and the mouth too large, even though it looked kind. His eyes were kind too, blue and heavy-lidded under thick arched brows a shade darker than his pale hair.

'Oh, dear!' she was breathless. 'I am sorry—you see I was on the late side and I didn't expect you.' She smiled at him, her rather plain but pleasant face suddenly pretty, her astonishing violet eyes—her one beauty—twinkling at him.

'If it comes to that,' said the man, 'I wasn't expecting you, either.' He smiled back at her. 'Don't let me keep you.'

She was already a few yards away when she wheeled back again. 'You're not hurt, are you?' she asked anxiously. 'If you are, I'll take you along to Cas. and someone will have a look at you.'

HARLEQUIN®

Mediterranean NIGHTS™

Experience glamour, elegance, mystery and revenge aboard the high seas....

Coming in September 2007...

BREAKING ALL THE RULES

by

Marisa Carroll

Aboard the cruise ship *Alexandra's Dream* for some R & R, sports journalist Lola Sandler is surprised to spot pro-golfer Eric Lashman. Years after walking away from the pro circuit with no explanation to the public, Eric now finds himself teaching aboard a cruise ship.

Lola smells a career-making exposé... but their developing relationship may force her to make a difficult choice.

www.eHarlequin.com HM38963

ATHENA FORCE

Heart-pounding romance and thrilling adventure.

Professional negotiator Lindsey Novak is faced with her biggest challenge—to buy back Teal Arnett, a young woman with unique powers. In the process Lindsey uncovers a devastating plot that involves scientists from around the globe, and all of them lead to one woman who is bent on destroying Athena Academy…at any cost.

LOOK FOR

THE GOOD THIEF

by Judith Leon

Available September wherever you buy books.

www.eHarlequin.com

AF38973

His mouth twitched. 'My dear young lady, yours is a very small bicycle and I, if you take a good look, am a very large man—eighteen stone or so. I hardly noticed it.'

She beamed her relief. 'Oh, good. 'Bye.'

She was off again, pedalling furiously for a side door, and because she was going to be late, she left her bike down the covered passage which led to the engineer's shop; she would ring them presently and ask one of them to take it round to the shed where the nurses were supposed to keep their bicycles; it wouldn't be the first time she had done it.

She still had some way to go; through the old part of the hospital, across the narrow alley separating it from the new wing, and then up several flights of stairs; she arrived at the swing doors which led to the theatre unit only very slightly out of breath, her face, with its small high-bridged nose and wide mouth, flushed by her exertions.

Sister Collins was in the changing room, buttoning her theatre dress. 'Almost late,' she commented as she went out, and Beth sighed as she tore out of her clothes. Sister Collins was the kind of person who said, 'Almost late,' when anyone else would have said, 'A minute to spare.'

Beth tucked her brilliant hair into the mob cap worn by theatre staff and made for the Recovery Room. There was a heavy list for the day and she wouldn't be off until half past four; she cast a regretful look out of the window at the blue sky and sunshine of the April morning outside—Chifney would be looking its best, she thought, on such a morning, but her old home belonged to her stepbrother now, and she hadn't seen it for a long time. Philip had inherited it when their father died, and neither she nor William, her younger brother, had been back since, not even for a holiday. Philip wouldn't exactly turn them out if they chose to go there, but he and his wife would make it quite plain that they were only there on sufferance. She remembered how, when they had been quite small, and he ten years older, he had been at pains to explain to them that their mother was their father's second wife and therefore they would have nothing at all when he died and that he, for his part, had no intention of giving them a home. He had always hated his stepmother, a quiet gentle woman who wouldn't have harmed a fly, and when she had died he had transferred his bitter dislike to herself and William.

And it had turned out exactly as he had said it would. Luckily William had been left just enough money to finish university and train as a doctor, and Beth, bent on being a nurse and having nowhere else to go, had joined forces with him, and for five years now had lived in a rather poky little flat in the more unfashionable part of London, SE. She had been left a tiny annuity too, which helped, especially as William was extravagant, and on the whole they managed quite well. William was doing his post-graduate years now and she had been a staff nurse for two years and there had been hints just lately that very shortly she would be offered a Sister's post. She had nothing to complain of, she assured herself as she went round methodically testing the oxygen, inspecting the trays and making sure that there was enough of everything to keep them going until the end of the list. Harriet King, the third-year nurse who worked with her, had already fetched the blood for the first case and was now, under Sister Collins' sharp eyes, setting out an injection tray. Beth picked up the theatre list, glanced at the clock and went off to fetch the first patient, a middle-aged lady from the Private Wing on the floor below, who, despite her pre-med., indulged, once she was on the trolley and in the lift, in an attack of screaming hysterics, which was rather overdoing things, seeing that she was only having a small nodule removed from one shoulder; a matter of five minutes' work by the surgeon and accompanied by no possible cause for alarm.

Beth soothed her as best she could, chatting about this and that and laying a surprisingly firm hand on the lady's well-upholstered front when she signified her intention of sitting up.

'Now, now,' said Beth soothingly, genuinely sorry for the poor scared woman, 'here's Mr Todd who is to give you the anaesthetic—you saw him yesterday, didn't you? I'm going to hold your hand and he'll give you the teeniest prick in your arm and you'll go to sleep at once.'

The patient started to protest, but Mr Todd had slipped in his needle and her eyes had closed before she could frame even one word.

'You're always so nice to them,' he said. 'Give me that tube, Beth—in the bad old days she would have gone to her local GP and he'd have done it under a local and no nonsense.'

She smiled at him behind her mask. 'But it isn't what's going to be done to you—that's all the same once you're under—it's the idea…'

She broke off to hand over to Theatre Staff Nurse, and with a cheerful little nod slid back into the Recovery Room; they would be ready in Theatre Two for their first case. She collected a porter and a trolley and set off once more, this time to Men's Surgical.

The morning slid quietly away and had become afternoon before there was a chance to get a meal, and then it was sandwiches and yoghurt sent up from the canteen. And the afternoon went even more quickly, with all four theatres going flat out and an emergency added on to the end of Theatre One's list just as Beth was starting to clear up. She would be home late again, and William, whose free evening it was, would have to wait for the dinner she had promised to cook for him. She was finished at last, though, and changed without much thought to her appearance and making her way out of the theatre block into the labyrinth of passages which took up the space behind the impressive entrance hall in the older part of the hospital. She was negotiating these when she saw her brother ahead of her. He was standing at the junction of four passages, talking to someone out of sight, which didn't prevent her cheerful: 'William—I'm only just off, so supper will be late. You'd better call in at the Black Dog and have a pint…' She had reached him by now and went on briskly: 'Why are you making that extraordinary face?'

There was no need for him to tell her; his out-of-sight companion came into view as she reached the corner—the man she had almost run down on her bike that morning. She smiled at him. 'Oh, hullo—is your back still OK?'

Seeing him for a second time she was struck by his size and by the fact that he wasn't as young as she had supposed him to be. 'You don't always feel it at first,' she explained kindly, and heard William draw in his breath sharply.

'This,' he said in his most reproving voice, 'is Professor van Zeust from Leyden University in Holland—he lectures in surgery.' His tone was reverent.

'Oh, do you?' Beth put out a hand and had it gently wrung. 'I had no idea.' Her engagingly plain face broke into a grin. 'And me telling you to go along to Cas.! You could have told me.'

'If you remember, you were already late,' he reminded her. His voice was kind, but she had the impression that he didn't want to waste time talking to her. She gave him a friendly nod, said, 'See you later, William,' and went on her way, aware that her brother wasn't best pleased with her.

He got to the flat an hour later, just as she was laying the table for their supper, and being a careless young man, he cast his books on one chair, his scarf on to another and himself into a third.

'You are a little idiot,' he began, 'talking like that to one of the most distinguished surgeons in Europe.'

Beth was at the stove, dishing up. 'Oh? Does he live on a pedestal or something? He seemed quite human to me.'

'Of course he's human,' her brother spoke testily, 'but he's…he should be respected…'

'But I was quite polite.'

He agreed reluctantly and went on: 'Yes, but do you know what he said after you'd gone? He wanted to know where you worked and then he said that you didn't appear to him to be quite like the other nurses he had met.'

Beth bore their plates to the table. 'Ah, he noticed how plain I am.'

'Well, I daresay,' William agreed with brutal candour, 'but he could have meant that you didn't treat him with enough respect.'

'Pooh,' said Beth with scorn, 'and you were chatty enough, the pair of you.'

William was attacking his supper in the manner of a starving man. 'I happened to meet him,' he said with a full mouth and great dignity, 'and he asked me to take a message about the times of his lectures.'

Beth gave him a second helping. 'I wonder where he lives?' she wanted to know.

'Haven't a clue. What's for pudding?'

After supper he left her to the washing up and went to his room to study, and when she expressed surprise at his sudden enthusiasm for work, he told her rather sheepishly that old van Zeust was a good enough fellow and knew how to give a lecture. 'Besides,' he went on, 'I happen to be interested in his particular line of work.' He gave her a lofty look as he left the room, although he was back again within five minutes to ask if she could lend him a fiver until the end of the month.

She went and fetched the money at once, for she was a good sister to him and moreover quite understood that young men needed money for beer and taking girls out. The fiver was part of a nest egg she had been saving towards some new clothes, and she very much doubted if she would get it back again. But William was a dear; he had been kind to her when they had left Chifney and he paid his half of the rent, even if he did borrow it back again within a week or so. In a year or two's time, when he had finished his post-graduate work and got himself a really good job, he would probably marry, and then she would have to find a smaller flat and live in it by herself—unless she got married too, and that didn't seem very likely; not now. If she had stayed at home and her father had been alive, she would have been Miss Partridge of Chifney House, and perhaps one of the young men living in the district, sons of small landowners, would have married her, for there she had been the daughter of the house and what she lacked in looks she had made up for with charm, so that she had had a great many friends. But here in London, no one cared who she was; it had taken her a little while to get used to the indifference of Londoners to each other, and indeed, she had discovered during the years that they had lived there that life in a city wasn't at all the same thing as life at Chifney—there, if you were ill, the whole village knew, willing helpers rallied round to feed the cat, mow the grass, leave delicious baked custards on the doorstep, fetch the children from school, and when her father had been alive he could always be depended upon to help out if funds were low. She very much doubted if her stepbrother did that.

The Dutch professor was in the theatre the next morning. The first case was a kidney transplant, to be done by Professor MacDonald, one of the leading men in that line of surgery. It was soon apparent that he and the Dutchman were old friends; Beth could hear their voices in the surgeons' changing room, the Scotsman's deliberate and a little gruff, his companion's deep and slow. They came out together presently and went into theatre, and when Beth went in with the patient they were scrubbed, standing facing each other across the operating table. The surgical registrar was scrubbed too and so were two house surgeons; the place teemed with white and green-clad figures. Beth, thinking of the long hours ahead, was glad that she didn't have to stay in theatre; she would be kept busy with patients from the other theatres and it would be later—much later—when she would come back to collect her patient once more. She handed him over now to the theatre staff and slipped away quickly to fetch the next case for Theatre Two.

It was hours later when she went to collect the kidney transplant. She was off duty at four-thirty again, but she saw that she could forget that; the man wasn't well and needed constant attention from both herself and Harriet King; besides that, his drain blocked and she had to buzz for the registrar, and while they were getting it to work again the patient stopped breathing, so that she had to leave the drain to him and begin resuscitation while someone went hot-foot for Professor MacDonald.

He came immediately, straight from the changing room bringing Professor van Zeust with him, still in their theatre trousers and vests, their caps on their heads. They might have looked faintly absurd if it hadn't been for their air of quiet authority.

It was a good deal later by the time the man was fit to move down to the Intensive Care Unit, and there was a great mass of clearing up to do after that. It was much later still when Beth crossed the courtyard on the way to fetch her bicycle and saw Professor van Zeust again. He looked quite different now; immaculate in a conventional, beautifully tailored suit. Out of the tail of her eye she saw him get into a massive Citroën CS, and decided that its size suited his vast proportions very nicely. He had gone by the time she had got her bike out and got back to the courtyard.

She didn't see him for several days after that; indeed, beyond an annoying persistence her mind had developed in thinking of him, he should have been, as it were, a closed book. It was William who made it difficult for her to make an end of him; he talked about the Dutchman incessantly, not only when he got home in the evenings when he was free to do so, but during their breakfasts together; a meal usually eaten at speed and with no more conversation than was absolutely necessary. The professor was, according to her brother, not at all a bad fellow—knew his stuff but didn't have a big head about it, and what was more, he had been a first-class rugger player.

'Doesn't he play any more?' asked Beth, swallowing bread and butter as fast as she could.

William gave her a withering look. 'Good lord, he's getting on for forty—at least, he's thirty-six, and that's pretty old.'

She supposed it was; in twelve years' time she would be that age herself, although forty in a man didn't sound old at all, whereas in a woman... She wondered with vague worry where she would be when she was forty. In all probability not married, for her looks were hardly likely to improve with age.

It was the following day after this not very satisfying conversation that the theatre was alerted for an emergency. They had had a busy morning and a break for dinner would be nice, so that there was an involuntary sigh when the Theatre Super, Miss Toms, put her head round the door with the news. 'Theatre One,' she said crisply. 'Miss Partridge, take one of the porters and go down to Private Wing—the patient is to come up at once. Acute appendix.'

Beth, half way out of her theatre dress, put it back on again. Miss Toms, fortyish, elegant and always polite, was obeyed by everyone, and that included the housemen, even at times the consultants, although they were probably unaware of it. She had a habit of addressing everyone by their correct names, too, which somehow made the theatre into a more human place to work in. She smiled at Beth now. 'You shall be relieved, as soon as possible,' she promised, 'but this is rather a special patient—Mevrouw Thorbecke, Professor van

Zeust's sister. I imagine he will be coming into theatre. Professor MacDonald will be operating.'

Beth nodded and Miss Toms sailed away to scrub up; she always scrubbed for staff or staff's family, and although the professor wasn't quite staff, his sister would be accorded the same treatment.

The patient was a pretty woman even though she was a sickly pale green and her fair hair was damp with sweat. She was game too, for she managed a smile as they got her on to the trolley, she even managed a murmured hullo and muttered in English: 'I didn't believe it but they *are* violet.' The remark mystified Beth, but there was so much to do just then that she forgot it immediately.

Miss Toms was right; Professor Van Zeust was in the anaesthetic room when they reached it, gowned and masked and talking to Professor MacDonald and Doctor Moore, the senior anaesthetist, but he didn't stay long, only to say something in a cheerful voice and in his own language to his sister. He didn't look at Beth at all.

It was a nasty appendix, on the point of perforation. The two men grunted with satisfaction when the offending thing had been removed and Professor MacDonald began to close the small wound. 'Who is looking after the brats?' he asked his companion.

The Dutchman snipped a suture thread. 'No time to make any arrangements—not yet. I'll have to get hold of someone, I suppose; Martina won't feel like coping with them for a few weeks. They're a match for anyone in the best of health, let alone for anyone a little under the weather.'

'When's Dirk due back?'

'Another six weeks.' He tossed the stitch scissors on to the Mayo's table and stood back a little. He smiled over his mask at Miss Toms and then said, 'Thanks, George, I'll hang around if I may.'

The two men went out together and Beth came from the corner where she had been waiting to take over the care of the patient. It was quiet in the Recovery Room; there were no other patients there, most of the staff were still at their dinner and Miss Toms, having performed her duties with the ease and perfection expected of her, had disappeared too. A theatre staff nurse and a student were getting the theatre ready once more for the afternoon list, in ten minutes or so the rest of them would be streaming back and the skeleton staff which had remained behind would be free to go to their dinners. But for the moment Beth was occupied with her patient; there was little enough to do, as she would be round in a few minutes—indeed, as Beth inspected the quiet face on the trolley, she could see a faint tremor of the eyelids, so that she began the usual routine of hand patting and 'Wake up, Mevrouw Thorbecke, it's all over, everything's fine.'

She had to do this several times before her patient

responded with a languid lifting of her eyelids and a mumbled word or two which made no sense at all.

Beth made her observations and charted them and looked at her carefully; she was quite fit to go back to the ward, but no patient might be sent back from the Recovery Room until they opened their eyes properly, told the nurse their name and could state if they were in pain or not.

'Are you in pain?' asked Beth in her nice quiet voice.

Mevrouw Thorbecke nodded, her eyes shut.

'I'll give you something for it. Will you tell me your name?'

'You know who I am—I wish to sleep.' Her voice was a mumble and a frown came and went. 'I have a pain.'

'OK,' said Beth, talking to herself, 'you shall have something now, though you're not really supposed to have it until you're quite round. Hang on a sec...'

Mevrouw Thorbecke mumbled crossly in her own language as Beth checked her pulse. The smallest of sounds behind her made her look over her shoulder. Professor van Zeust was standing quite close, leaning against one of the trolleys and her eyes brightened at the sight of him. 'Oh, what luck that you should turn up just when I could do with you,' she exclaimed sunnily, and he, who had been there all the time, smiled a little.

'You need help?' he inquired mildly.

'Well, Mevrouw Thorbecke is almost round and we're not supposed to give a post-op. until the patient is quite conscious, but now you're here, perhaps you'd give me the all clear to give her some Pethedine before she goes downstairs. She's quite OK, but not quite with us yet.'

The professor's mouth twitched just a little. 'I'll take the responsibility, Staff Nurse—ram home whatever you've got there and get her down to the ward, will you? Doctor Moore asked me to look in; he was called away to some emergency.'

He walked unhurriedly over to the trolley and took his sister's pulse and when she opened an unwilling eye said something to her in a soft voice. 'She's fine,' he declared, and went away so quietly that Beth didn't realize that he had gone.

She delivered her patient, drowsy now, to the Ward Sister on the Private Wing and sped back to the Recovery Room. Sister Collins and Harriet would be back in a matter of minutes; she started to clear up with Mrs Wise, the orderly, to help her and they were just finished when the other two returned.

The afternoon went quickly after that, but then it nearly always did, there was always so much to do. The list was a long one and although Beth was due off at half past seven, it was considerably later than that when at last she left the theatre.

It had been William's half day and she was surprised and touched to find that he had laid the table and made a few rather inadequate preparations for supper.

He followed her into the kitchen while she cooked it, something he seldom did, so that she asked: 'Aren't you going out? You usually do on your half day—did Wendy stand you up?'

Wendy was the current young lady of his fancy; she was a physiotherapist whom no one liked much because she gave herself airs, but Beth had suffered an unending catalogue of her perfections with sisterly patience, knowing that within a week or two her brother's eye would have been caught by some other girl. They were all alike, the young doctors and students, and no one took them seriously, although a few fell permanently in love and got engaged or even married. But William would be too busy for the next year or so to think about marrying; he had only just got started on his career and at the end of his six months with Professor MacDonald's firm he would be joining the medical side if they would have him, and after that it would be a year—two years, at least, before he could apply for a post as registrar. She dished up their meal and carried it through to the sitting-room while he explained that Wendy hadn't stood him up; he had decided to stay home because he wanted to talk to her.

'Me?' exclaimed Beth, much astonished at this brotherly attention. 'Whatever for? I haven't any money till payday...'

William frowned. 'It's not that,' he said impatiently.

'You've got a week's holiday starting on Sunday, haven't you, Beth?' He sounded uneasy all at once.

She began her supper and then paused to pour their coffee. 'Yes—fancy you remembering that. But it's only Tuesday you know, and I'm not going anywhere. Do you want the flat to yourself or something?'

'Don't be dim. The thing is, if you've nothing to do I know of someone who wants to borrow you...'

'Borrow me? Whatever for? Anyway, I'm on holiday—is it one of those agencies?'

'No, as a matter of fact, it's Professor van Zeust. You had his sister in theatre today, didn't you? Well, he's been left high and dry with her four children; they're staying with him. He mentioned it to old Mac, and he knew—lord knows how—that you had a holiday coming up, and he suggested that you might step into the breach—just for a week, you know, and look after them. You'd be paid.'

Beth's bosom swelled with indignation. 'Well, whatever next—why me? Aren't there agencies for nannies and mothers' helps? Why can't he go to one of them? I've no intention...'

She caught William's eye and something in it made her say: 'You wretch—you said I would!' She drew a deep breath, her eyes very purple, but before she could speak he said hastily:

'Oh, be a sport, Beth—after all, you're not doing anything and it might be fun.'

'Fun?' Her voice was shrill with annoyance. 'Have you ever looked after four children? They're not even English!' She paused and added triumphantly: 'So I can't.'

'They've had an English nanny for years. I don't know much about it, but I believe they live somewhere behind Harrods—quite super, and you're bound to get heaps of free time.' He looked at her anxiously. 'It's only for a week.'

She stared at him across the table. 'And supposing I should decide to do it, who is going to tell me what and when and where?'

He brightened. 'Professor van Zeust said he'd make a point of seeing you tomorrow—there's another kidney transplant, isn't there? I shall be in theatre too,' he paused to contemplate this pleasure, then went on: 'There's sure to be an opportunity to talk about it. I say, Beth, it would be jolly decent of you if you would, it'd do me a good turn—I mean, they're more likely to remember me later on if there was the chance of a registrar's job.'

Beth got up and started to collect the dishes. 'Well, dear, I'm not going to say yes now, but I do promise to have an open mind if he says anything to me about it tomorrow, though probably he'll have got someone else by then.'

But while she washed up she found herself hoping that the professor wouldn't be able to find anyone else, even though before she went to bed she told William firmly that she hadn't made up her mind…all the same, when she got into bed, she stayed awake quite a long while thinking about him.

CHAPTER TWO

BETH was on duty at eight o'clock the following morning and within a very short time the theatre was in full swing. She had fetched the kidney transplant case—a young girl in her teens—handed her over and gone again to collect the first of a long list of cases for the other theatres. The kidney case lasted a long time; it was early afternoon before she received the girl in the Recovery Room and although Professor van Zeust came with his colleague to see her, he had nothing to say other than a few quiet directions. They went away presently and later, after Beth had taken her case to ICU, an emergency came in and she was kept busy until some time after she was due off duty. Of the professor there was no sign, and she left the hospital feeling a bit let down; he might at least have given her the chance of refusing the job which he had so surprisingly suggested she might take. True, there had been no time to say anything at all for most of the day, but he could have left a message. Probably he had found someone else after all and forgotten about the whole thing.

She arrived at the flat rather cross, and over a cup of tea decided that nothing would persuade her to take the job now, even if he begged her to, and as this was highly unlikely she stopped thinking about it, drained the teapot, ate a piece of toast left over from breakfast, and fell to washing the smalls before getting the supper. William would be home shortly, before going back to St Elmer's at ten o'clock to be on call for twenty-four hours, and he would be hungry, as usual. It was unfortunate that the kitty was at a low ebb, but it always was just before pay day. She settled on a macaroni cheese, made it rather impatiently and went to her room to tidy herself.

The flat, the top floor of a Victorian house which had seen better days, was cramped and a bit dark and her room was small and cramped too, but she rather liked the view over the chimneypots; it was better than the houses opposite and the sky gave her a feeling of space. She wasted a few minutes now, looking out and thinking about Chifney, where there were only trees and fields, and the chimney-pots, when visible, fitted cosily into the scenery around them. Her room was nicely furnished, though, with bits and pieces her step-brother had allowed them to take with them when they had left home, and she kept the flat sparklingly clean and somehow managed to have flowers in it.

She brushed her hair and tied it back, so that it hung in a thick shower down her back, re-did her face without much enthusiasm, not seeing her lovely eyes and splendid hair, only the ordinariness of her features, then twitched and pulled her brown tweed skirt and sweater into place. She was heartily sick of them both, but William needed shoes again and the money he had been saving for them he had spent, naturally enough, he conceded, on a wildly expensive waistcoat; she would have to help him out and put off buying a new outfit for herself for just a little longer.

She wandered back to the sitting room, shook up a few cushions and then pottered into the kitchen to see how the macaroni cheese was coming along. When the front door bell rang she banged the oven door shut with a touch of irritation and went to answer it, with a rather cross: 'You've forgotten your key again…'

Only it wasn't William, it was Professor van Zeust, looming over her in the narrow doorway. She peered round him as far as she could, and quite forgetful of her manners, demanded: 'Where's William?'

His bland: 'Good evening, Miss Partridge,' reminded her of them.

'Oh, good evening, Professor. I'm sorry—I didn't mean to be rude—I thought you were William. Have you come to see him? He's late, I'm afraid, but if you would like to come in and wait?'

He smiled down at her. 'William has had to fill in

for the Casualty Officer. He asked me to tell you that he won't be home tonight.'

'Oh.' She stood uncertainly. 'Then why—that is...' She stopped, not quite sure what to say next. After all, he was a consultant, an important man at the hospital and probably even more important in his own country, and she wasn't sure how she should address a professor off duty.

'If I might come in?' His voice was pleasantly friendly.

'Of course. You—you took me rather by surprise.' She led the way into the sitting room and he paused on its threshold and looked about him with interest, drawing an appreciative breath as he did so. 'Toasted cheese?' he inquired.

'Supper,' she told him succinctly, and waved a well kept hand towards a chair, then sat down herself, waiting patiently for him to say whatever it was he had to say.

'Your brother was kind enough to tell Professor McDonald that you might consider looking after my sister's children while she is in hospital,' he began without any beating about the bush, 'but before I say any more, I should like to know if the suggestion is agreeable to you. I understand from Professor MacDonald that you have a week's holiday and I feel bound to point out that the job is no sinecure. I had intended applying to an agency for some sort of help, but I should very much prefer that it should be someone whom I know.'

'But you don't know me.'

'You are thought of very highly at St Elmer's, and I have seen for myself that you don't flap.'

Beth blinked at him. 'Are they the sort of children who might make one flap?' she asked forthrightly.

He burst out laughing. 'Perhaps, they need firm handling. What do you say?'

She studied him carefully. He was nice; never mind that he was one of the best-looking men she had ever met, never mind the charm of his smile and his deep, quiet voice; he would have been just as nice if he had had a squint and outstanding ears. His hair, she noticed, was grey at the temples and his eyes were very blue. 'All right,' she said quietly, 'I'll take them on. I'd like to know something about them though, and does your sister want me to live in or go each day?'

'Oh, if you would live there, I think, and regarding your fee...' he mentioned a sum which sent her arched brows flying upwards.

'But that's heaps too much—four times as much as nannies and people like that get.'

'But you will have four times as much as that to do.' He spoke firmly and she had the feeling that if she were to argue he would get annoyed.

'Very well, thank you.' She smiled across at him. 'Would you like a cup of coffee?'

His reply astonished her. 'I should like to stay to supper,' he said.

She hadn't been Miss Partridge of Chifney House for nothing, she hastened to invite him with just the right degree of pleasure and served the simple meal with an aplomb which would have done justice to something far more elaborate. 'I'm afraid there's no beer,' she informed her guest, 'but there's orange squash…'

The professor assured her that orange squash was exactly what he would have chosen and when Beth poured him a glass of this innocuous beverage, drank it with every sign of enjoyment, he ate his portion of macaroni cheese with a flattering appetite too, talking gently about this and that, so that she hardly realized that she was answering any number of skilfully put questions. By the time they were drinking their coffee she had told him quite a lot about Chifney as well as revealing, quite unknowingly, a good deal about her stepbrother.

'You have a pleasant home here,' remarked the professor, and sounded as though he meant it, 'and some delightful pieces of furniture.'

'Aren't they? Philip allowed us to bring them with us, you know. They don't quite suit the flat, but we grew up with them.' She poured more coffee for them both, feeling wonderfully at ease with this large, quiet man. She would have liked to have told him so many things and might have done so if she hadn't reminded herself with her usual good sense that all good medical men had the power of making one feel at ease and able to talk freely. She frowned, hoping she hadn't talked too much; perhaps she should change the conversation.

'You were going to tell me something about your nephews and nieces,' she prompted him.

'Ah, yes—but first I think we should wash up.'

'Wash up? Good heavens, no! I'm sure you've never washed up in your life.'

He smiled faintly. 'I wonder what makes you think that?' His voice held a note of inquiry and she flushed a little.

'I didn't mean to sound rude,' she assured him, 'and I can do it later.'

For answer he began to pile the plates tidily and carried them through to the kitchen, and it struck her that he was a man who, once he had made up his mind, didn't like it changed for him. They washed up together, talking in a casual friendly way which she found very pleasant, then went back to the sitting room, where the professor settled himself in a chair again with the air of one staying for the rest of the evening.

'About the children,' he began, 'the eldest is Dirk, he's ten, then there is Marineka, who is eight, Hubert, seven and Alberdina, the littlest, who is five. They are normal healthy children, that is to say they are as naughty and disobedient as most children of their ages. On the whole their manners are passable, they don't sulk and I should say that they have a strong sense of fair play. They adore their mother, who spoils them, and hero-worship their father, an archaeologist of some repute, at present somewhere in Chile leading an expedition of some sort or other. He will be away for several more weeks, and since I had already accepted an invitation from St Elmer's to give a series of lectures, Martina—my sister—decided that it would be a good idea if they were to come over to England at the same time. The children, by the way, speak tolerable English; they had an English nanny until she left to get married a short time ago.' He paused to smile. 'You are still willing to come?'

Beth's wide mouth turned up its corners in a delightful smile. 'Oh, yes. When do you want me to start?'

'I am told that your holiday starts on Sunday.' He paused to ask if he might light his pipe and Beth sat composedly watching him, saying nothing, and presently he went on: 'There is a housekeeper and daily help, but they aren't suitable for the children—besides, they have enough to do. You would have to be with them for most of the day, although I will undertake to have them with me if and when I am there. You are prepared for that?'

'Yes, of course,' she assured him. What was curtailed freedom when it meant William's new shoes and some clothes for herself as well? 'I've days off on Friday and Saturday. I could go along on Friday afternoon if you would like that. Where am I to go?'

He scribbled an address in his pocket book, tore out

the page, and handed it to her. 'Take a taxi,' he advised her, 'your expenses will be paid.'

She glanced at the address he had written down and then looked again because his writing was almost illegible. William had been right, it was somewhere close to Harrods—a rented house, presumably—possibly someone he knew; doctors helped each other... She was aware that he had got to his feet and jumped up briskly. 'It was kind of you to come—I quite thought you had found someone else.'

She smiled as she spoke, but he answered seriously: 'No—you seemed so suitable, and Professor MacDonald thinks highly of you—I am sure that I could have done no better.'

She found this speech a little damping, so that her good-bye was stiff, but once she had shut the door on his broad back, she whisked to William's bedroom window which overlooked the street, and looked cautiously out, in time to see him getting into the Citroën. She craned her neck in order to get a better view; he must be very successful if he could afford to run a car costing almost seven thousand pounds, even though it matched his size. It was disconcerting when he looked up and caught her peering down, and waved.

Beth got up early on Friday morning, gave William his breakfast and a list of instructions which she knew very well he wouldn't attend to, and set about cleaning the flat. William, though willing, was unhandy about the house and it would probably be in a shocking state when she got back, but at least she could leave it in apple pie order. She sighed as she Hoovered; a holiday—a real holiday—would have been super, but she cheered herself up with the promise of the shopping expedition she would have—a new suit, she decided happily while she packed a few things in a case; the despised skirt and sweater, a suede jerkin to wear over them if the days proved cool, a raincoat and a jersey dress; the only decent one she had, leaf green and simple enough for it not to matter that it was a year old at least, slacks, she supposed, and a shirt-blouse. She would wear her suit, a bargain in the January sales, Irish tweed and well cut, and she had her good leather shoes and handbag. She dressed quickly, did her face and hair, picked up her case and went downstairs to telephone for a taxi; it wasn't the sort of neighbourhood where one was easily to be found.

The address which the professor had given her was just off Sloane Square; a quiet cul-de-sac reached by a narrow street and lined on three sides by tall elegant houses. There was an enclosed garden in its centre and it had all the peace of a country village. Very Knightsbridge, thought Beth, paying the driver before picking up her case and ascending the steps of number three.

The door was opened before she could ring the bell. A small, cheerful-faced woman wished her good day and without asking her what her business was, stood aside for her to go in. 'You'll be Miss Partridge,' she declared comfortably, 'the professor said you'd be arriving about now. If you'll put your case down someone will bring it to your room presently, miss. I thought you might like to go there straight away and then have a cup of tea. The children are in the park with Nelly, who comes in to help most days; that'll give you time to look around you. This way, if you please.'

She led the way down the narrow elegant hall to the staircase, curving up from its end wall. Half-way up she paused to get her breath, for she was on the stout side. 'Your room's on the second floor, with the children, miss; the professor thought it might be nicer for you as well as easier.' She beamed kindly at Beth, who smiled back, liking her, before they went on again, across a surprisingly wide landing and up another flight of stairs opening on to a semicircle of thick carpet, lighted by a big bow window and with several doors leading from it. The housekeeper opened the first of these, disclosing a good sized room, furnished tastefully with Regency mahogany and curtained and carpeted in a delicate shade of blue.

'Oh, charming!' exclaimed Beth, quite carried away with the idea of having it for her own for a week; it reminded her of her room at Chifney's, only there were no fields to be seen from its window, only the treetops from the little square in front of the house. She turned to smile again at her companion. 'You must be the housekeeper—may I know your name?'

'Mrs Silver, miss. I've been housekeeper here for many years now, ever since the professor inherited this house from his grandfather—that was his mother's father, her being English. He's not here all that often, not having the time, being such a busy gentleman.'

She turned round as a thin youngish woman appeared in the doorway with Beth's case. 'And this is Miss Powers; she comes in daily to help and what a blessing that is, I can tell you.' She nodded and smiled and went on: 'And now we'll leave you to unpack your things, then perhaps you'll come downstairs when you're ready, there'll be a nice tea ready for you. Would ten minutes suit you, miss?'

Beth thanked her and fell to unpacking, a task quickly accomplished so that she had time to tidy her hair and re-do her face and take a closer look at the room. It was really quite beautiful; the professor's grandfather must have been a man of excellent taste. She looked around her as she made her way downstairs too, and found the same elegance, and promised herself a closer inspection of the pictures hanging on the walls when she had the leisure—if she had any leisure; the professor had warned her that she would have her hands full.

Mrs Silver appeared in the hall as Beth trod the last stair and led the way across the hall and opened a door, inviting her to enter, adding that tea would be brought in a very few minutes. Beth murmured her thanks, wishing to ask if there really was time for her to have tea before the children arrived, but Mrs Silver had already gone, closing the door silently behind her, leaving Beth to look around her.

It was a large, comfortably furnished room, two button-backed sofas flanked the marble fireplace, and there were a variety of easy chairs scattered about, as well as a Sheraton sofa table, a number of lamp tables and a handsome display cabinet against one wall. There were pictures on its panelled walls, too; she began a leisurely tour of them, craning her neck to see those above her head and retracing her steps to take another look at something she had liked. She had reached the fireplace by now and tiptoed to study the portrait above it—bewhiskered old gentleman, smiling a little, with heavy-lidded blue eyes.

'That'll be Grandfather,' Beth told herself aloud. 'He looks an old poppet—he's got the same eyes too.' She turned with a smothered shriek at the chuckle behind her. Deep in the recesses of a porter's chair, half turned away from the room, sat the professor, watching her.

'You're quite right,' he observed blandly, 'we do share the same eyes and he was—what was the word?— an old poppet.' He got up as he spoke and came towards her. 'Unpardonable of me to remain silent, was it not? But if you had turned this way you would have seen me.'

'Yes—well I didn't expect you to be here.' She was a little indignant.

'I didn't expect to be here either, but the last case fell through and it occurred to me that it might be easier for you if I were here to introduce you and the children.' His kind smile came and went. 'Do sit down, Miss Partridge. Mrs Silver will be here at any moment with tea—I seldom have the chance to have it at home, and still less to share it with a such a delightful companion.'

Beth frowned horribly, aware that she had gone a bright pink, and he asked in a matter-of-fact way: 'You do not care for compliments? I assure you that I meant what I said.'

'Of course I like compliments,' she spoke a trifle crossly, 'all girls do, only I never quite believe them. You see, my face...you must have noticed I'm rather plain...'

His heavy lids drooped still further over his eyes and if she had hoped, deep down, that he would disclaim this bald statement, she was to be disappointed, for all he said was: 'I would have thought that it could be quite an asset in these days, when girls wear their prettiness like a uniform.'

She shook her head. 'Not for me, though I know what you mean, but there are some quite beautiful girls around.'

'Ah, beauty is quite a different matter and there aren't all that number, you know.'

'There's a very beautiful girl on the Surgical

Block,' Beth told him. 'Maureen Brooks, you're bound to see her while you're at St Elmer's—she's super; black hair and...'

'She lisps.'

'Oh, you've met her already. Most people think a lisp's rather nice.'

He looked amused. 'My dear Miss Partridge, has somebody told you that I am still a bachelor? I assure you that I am very content to be so, and although I am sure that you mean to be helpful, I'm quite able to find myself a wife should I wish for one.'

She went scarlet and jumped out of the chair where she had perched herself. 'You know very well that I didn't mean anything of the sort,' she declared indignantly. 'As a matter of fact, I didn't know you weren't married, although,' she added honestly, 'I thought perhaps you weren't.'

The professor had got to his feet too, standing so close to her that she was forced to put her head back to see his face. 'Perhaps I won't do,' she stated flatly.

He gave a crack of laughter. 'Of course you're going to do—the children will like you, I'm sure of it, and I could think of no one I would rather have to look after them. You're a nice change from the usual girl, Miss Partridge; it's pleasant to meet a girl who is different.'

He went back to his chair. 'And now sit down again, dear girl, here is tea at last, and if it makes you happier we will discuss the weather or some such topic, which will be very dull but should guarantee us not arguing.'

But there was no need for them to talk about anything as mundane; they fell to discussing books and music and a surprisingly large number of other subjects which they found they had in common, although Beth, munching her way daintily through anchovy toast, sandwiches and a rich chocolate cake, noticed that he kept the conversation impersonal; at the end of it she was just as ignorant as to where he lived in Holland and where he worked as she had ever been. Not, she thought vaguely, that that mattered in the slightest, for he would be going back to his own country very shortly, no doubt, and it could be of no consequence to her where he went or what he did.

Tea had been eaten and cleared away before the children arrived back. They came rushing in, all talking at once and in Dutch, making a beeline for their uncle, who sat back in his chair, apparently unworried by their delighted onslaught upon his vast person. It was only after they had talked themselves to a standstill that he said in English: 'I told you that while your mama was in hospital I would find someone to look after you all. This is Miss Elizabeth Partridge, who will do just that. Say how do you do and shake hands with her, if you please.'

He had told Beth that they were as disobedient as most children, but not at that particular moment they weren't. They came forward in turn to do as their uncle had bidden them, saying, 'How do you do?' and giving their names with almost old-fashioned good manners.

'How nice to meet you all,' declared Beth, beaming down at them all, 'and do you suppose that you might call me Beth? I should much prefer it.'

The professor had got to his feet; now he had done his duty in introducing the children to her, it seemed that he now felt free to go. 'Why not?' he agreed placidly. 'Do whatever Miss Partridge asks of you, my dears. Now I have an evening engagement and will bid you all good night, for you will be asleep by the time I get home. I shall see you tomorrow, no doubt.'

Left alone with the children, Beth sat down again and invited them to tell her about themselves, something they were ready enough to do and which gave her the opportunity to observe them rather more closely. Dirk, the obvious leader of the quartet, was tall for his age, fair-haired and blue-eyed and thin as only boys of ten can be. Marineka, who came next, was blue-eyed and fair-haired too and almost as tall as Dirk, although a good deal plumper, and Hubert was nicely chubby too, with the same ash-blond hair. It was the littlest one, Alberdina, who wasn't like any of them; she was short and decidedly plump, with large dark eyes and long brown hair. She could be only just five, Beth decided, for she still had a babyish way of sidling close and holding any hand which happened to present itself.

She was holding Beth's hand now, smiling up at her and saying something in Dutch.

'You have to speak English, Alberdina,' Dirk told her, and then explained: 'We all know how, because we had a nanny, but she's married now, and Alberdina hasn't had as much time to learn it as we have.'

'You all speak English beautifully,' Beth hastened to assure him. 'I only wish I could speak Dutch. And now will you tell me what you do now? Have you had your tea? And what do you do before bedtime?'

They all told her, so that it took her a little while to discover that they had their supper at six o'clock and then, starting with Alberdina, they went to bed—Dirk last of all at eight o'clock. 'Although sometimes I go to bed earlier than that,' he took pains to tell her, 'so that I can read, and of course on Saturdays, while we are here with Uncle Alexander, we stay up later.'

'What fun—why?'

'We go out with him in the afternoon, to the Zoo or for a ride in his car, and then we have tea somewhere special, and when we come home we play cards. We're good at cards. You play also?'

'Well, yes, though I'm not very good, I'm afraid, but I don't expect…that is, I daresay your uncle would like to have you to himself.'

They all nodded agreement so cheerfully that she felt quite disappointed.

It was evident that they were on their best behaviour; they took Beth over the house, much larger than it looked from the outside, showing her everything, even the cupboards and attics. They would have shown her their mother's room as well as their uncle's if she had given them the smallest encouragement. She declined a conducted tour of the kitchen too, merely asking where it was, just in case she should need to go there, though that seemed unlikely because Mrs Silver, stopping for a chat when she came to call the children to their supper, informed her in a kindly way that she was expected to do nothing at all save be with the children. 'And a great relief that will be to us all, miss, if I might say so—dear little things though they are and quite unnaturally quiet this evening, but that's because you're here. It will be nice to be able to get on with our work knowing they're in good hands.' With which heartening words, she nodded and smiled and went off to the kitchen.

Supper was in a small room at the back of the house, given up to the children's use while they were staying there. It was a pleasant place, furnished comfortably and obviously well lived in. Beth, presiding over the supper table, pouring hot chocolate and cutting up Alberdina's scrambled egg on toast into small pieces, found herself enjoying the children's company; it was a nice change to talk about fast cars, the dressing of dolls and the star footballers instead of the everlasting shop which was talked at the hospital, and even when she was home, William liked to tell her about his cases; many a meal she had eaten to the accompaniment of a blow-by-blow account of the appendix which had ruptured, the ulcer which had perforated on the way to theatre, the stitching he had been allowed to do…it was pleasant to forget all that and listen to the children's chatter. To sit at such a table with children such as these, but her own, watching them gobble with healthy appetites, hearing their high, clear voices, would be wonderful, she thought wistfully. She was deep in a daydream when she was roused by Hubert's asking why her eyes were a different colour from everyone else's.

'I don't really know,' she told him. 'It's just that they're mauve—everyone has different coloured eyes…'

'We all have blue eyes,' said Dirk, 'not Alberdina, of course, hers are brown, but Mama and Papa have blue eyes too and so has Uncle Alexander.'

'My doll, Jane, has brown eyes,' Marineka tossed her fair hair over her shoulder. 'It is to do with genes,' she announced importantly.

Beth looked at the little girl with something like awe. She hadn't known anything about genes until she was in the sixth form of the rather old-fashioned school her father had sent her to, but then of course she hadn't a doctor for an uncle and her father, moreover, hadn't held with girls knowing too much. She said hastily, before she became involved in a conversation concerning

genetics in which she felt reasonably sure she would
make but a poor show: 'Have you any pets at home?'

It was a successful red herring; there were several
cats, all with outlandish Dutch names, and a dog called
Rufus, as well as a tame rabbit or so, goldfish in a pond
in the garden and a canary, although the latter belonged
to someone called Mies whose function in their home
was not explained to her. It was an easy step from that
for Dirk to describe his uncle's two dogs, Gem and
Mini, black labradors, and when Beth commented on
their names, he gave her a sharp look. 'They're twins,'
he told her, and waited.

'Oh, I see—Gemini, the heavenly twins! Very clever
of someone to have thought of that.'

Her worth had obviously increased in his eyes. 'Not
many people think of that. Uncle Alexander has a cat
too, called Mops and two horses as well as a donkey,
and there's a pond with ducks. We feed them when we
go to stay with him.'

It would have been nice to have heard more, but what
would be the good? It would only stir up a vague feeling
which she supposed was envy. She suggested mildly
that it was about time Alberdina went to her bed, and
offered to help her take a bath, a suggestion which was
received with such a lack of surprise that she concluded
that the children were quite in the habit of having
someone to look after them; no wonder the professor
had been so anxious to find a substitute for their mother.

By half past eight they were tucked up, the two boys sharing a large room next to her own, the little girls across the landing. Beth, a little untidy after her exertions, retired to her room to change her sweater for a blouse and do her hair and face before going downstairs. Mrs Silver had said dinner at half past eight, and she was hungry.

It was lonely, though, after the bustle and noise of the hospital canteen, sitting at the oval table in the quiet dining room, with only Mrs Silver popping in and out with a succession of delicious foods, accompanying each dish with the strong encouragement to eat as much as she could. 'For I do hear that those hospitals don't feed their nurses all that well. Stodge, I daresay, miss—I don't hold with all that starch; here's a nice little soufflé, as light as a feather even though I do say it myself, you just eat it up.'

She trotted off again, with the advice that she would bring coffee to the sitting room in ten minutes' time, and left Beth to eat up the soufflé and then dash upstairs to make sure that all the children were asleep. They were; she went down to the sitting room and drank her coffee, and then, feeling guiltily idle, went to examine the book shelves which filled one wall. Early bed, she decided, and a book; there was a splendid selection for her to choose from.

She was trying to decide between the newest Alistair Maclean and Ira Morris's *Troika Belle*, which she had read several times already, when she heard steps in the hall and turned, a book in each hand, as the door opened and the professor came in.

He looked magnificent; a black tie did something for a man—it certainly did something for him. Not that he needed it, for he had the kind of looks which could get away with an old sweater and shapeless slacks, though Beth very much doubted if he ever allowed himself to be seen in such gear.

'Presumably the sight of me has rendered you speechless,' he commented dryly. 'I've wished you good evening twice and all I get is a blank purple stare.'

She put the books down and came into the centre of the room. 'I'm sorry…I was thinking. Is this your special room? Would you like me to go?'

'My dear good girl, of course not. My study is at the back of the hall—out of bounds to the children, but consider yourself invited to make use of it whenever you wish—only don't touch my desk.'

She smiled widely. 'Is it a mess? Doctors seem to like them that way. I was going up to bed, actually. The children have been splendid—and how good they are at their English, even Alberdina.' She made her way to the door. 'I rather think they wake early in the morning and I want to be ready for them.'

He had taken up a position before the empty fireplace, his eyes on her face. 'I've some messages from

Martina about the children, could you sit down for a minute while I pass them on?'

'Yes, of course.' She perched on the edge of a large chair and folded her hands in her lap. 'I hope Mevrouw Thorbecke is getting on well?'

'Excellently.' He pressed the old-fashioned bell by the fireplace and took a chair opposite hers. 'I've been to a very dull dinner party, do you mind if I have some coffee and something to eat?' He broke off as Mrs Silver came into the room.

They were obviously on the best of terms, for she clucked at him in a motherly fashion and burst at once into speech. 'There, Professor, didn't I know it—you were given a bad dinner and now you're famished,' and when he admitted that this was so: 'You just sit there and I'll bring you some coffee and sandwiches. I daresay Miss Partridge could drink another cup and keep you company.'

'Of course,' he said, before Beth could get her mouth open; Mrs Silver had gone by the time she managed: 'I had coffee after dinner, thank you.'

'You would prefer something else?' His voice was blandly charming.

'No, thanks.' She spoke firmly and wondered how it was that ten minutes later she was sitting there with a cup of coffee in her hand, and moreover, eating a sandwich. She was still there an hour later; she had forgotten that her companion was someone who, in the ordinary way, she would have addressed as sir, taken his word for law in theatre, and if she had encountered him outside their working sphere, wished him a sedate time of day and nothing more; she only knew that she was content to sit in his company, listening to his mild nothings and replying in kind. The handsome ormolu clock on the mantelpiece chiming the hour recalled her to the astonishing fact that it was midnight.

'Heavens, I never meant to stay as long as this,' she exclaimed, aware of regret as she jumped to her feet and made for the door. The professor had got to his feet too and with his hand on the door she stopped short.

'The messages,' she exclaimed again, 'you had some messages for me.'

He opened the door. 'I am ashamed to say that I have forgotten every one of them—they couldn't have been of much importance, could they? Your room is comfortable? You have everything you want?'

She told him yes, feeling a little uneasy about the messages, but there seemed nothing she could do about them now, so she wished him a good night and went to her room, where later, and still very wide awake, she thought about the evening, telling herself at the same time that it was only because she had been feeling lonely that she had found his company so very pleasant.

CHAPTER THREE

BETH took the children to Hyde Park in the morning and now that they had got used to her, a little of their natural high spirits were apparent; they screamed and laughed and ran races and fell over like any other child, and Beth, with no one much around to see, ran races too, her hair tumbling loose from her topknot and her cheeks flushed a healthy pink. And because it was such a lovely day, they walked home instead of taking the bus, with a good deal of stopping on the way to look at anything interesting which caught the eye of anyone in the party. They arrived on the doorstep in a happy chattering bunch and Beth rang the bell. It was the professor who opened the door to them and was instantly assailed by all four children, each telling their own version of the morning's amusements, interlarded with loud declarations of hunger. He suffered them with good-natured patience, giving his opinion on anything he was asked, and behaving, Beth was glad to see, just as an uncle should, and when he looked over their heads to ask her if she had enjoyed herself too, she answered happily enough. 'Oh, rather—it was super.'

'Beth's hair fell down,' piped Alberdina. 'She ran races, too, but she never won.'

'She's a girl,' said Dirk kindly, and the professor smiled faintly.

'I daresay that after a morning with this lot, Miss Partridge, you feel worn out. A glass of sherry before lunch, perhaps.'

She accepted, adding the proviso that it would have to be in a few minutes' time. 'I'll just get them upstairs and tidied—and me too,' she told him. 'Would five minutes do?'

'Admirably—I shall be in the sitting room.'

The children, she was quick to see, as once more neat as a new pin she sat sipping her sherry, were as good as gold; not only did they like their uncle very much, they had a healthy respect for him too. They sat quietly, Alberdina on her uncle's knee, the others in a row on one of the sofas, and although they took part in the conversation, they didn't make nuisances of themselves. Nanny must have been a paragon; Beth wondered uneasily if she had ever run races with the children in Hyde Park.

They were half-way through lunch when the professor mentioned in his placid way that he had wondered, as it was such a pleasant afternoon, if the children would like to go for a drive in the car. 'With tea, of course,' he finished amidst an excited outcry from his small relations.

'And Miss Partridge?' he wanted to know. 'Do you care to come with us? Saturday afternoon, you know.'

Beth hesitated; it would be delightful to accept, on the other hand was he just being polite? She glanced quickly at the faces round her; the children at least looked pleased with the idea, and when she peeped at the professor, there was nothing in his face to suggest that he minded one way or the other. 'Well—' she said slowly, and was drowned by the children's demands that she should go with them. 'If you want to,' she said a little shyly.

'We shall be delighted to have your company, Miss Partridge. Shall we say half past two, then?'

The children were brushed and combed and buttoned into their coats much too soon, which gave her a little time to attend to her own person. She would have to wear the suit, for she had nothing else which would do, but at least she could do her hair again and do the best she could with her face. Wholly dissatisfied with the result, she went downstairs, the children strung out behind her, and found the professor sitting on the wall table in the hall, smoking his pipe. When he saw them he got up and went to the kitchen door and sent a subdued shout to Mrs Silver that they would be out for tea and he would be out for dinner as well, before mar-shalling his party out of the front door and into the car.

They went to Hampton Court gardens, where they explored every aspect of the grounds before forming two groups and entering the maze. Beth, with Dirk and Marineka, was a little nervous of getting lost, so that it was with real relief that she found herself at the centre, although she wasn't at all sure how she had managed it. The professor, whom she strongly suspected already knew the way, was already there with Alberdina and Hubert, and after that getting out again, following each other in single file, was an easy matter.

They had tea in Richmond, the sort of tea children expected when they were taken out; hot buttered toast and sandwiches and plates of cakes. It was a merry meal with a good deal of laughing and talking, but at length the children could eat no more.

'Home,' the professor pronounced firmly. 'I've a date this evening, and one mustn't keep the ladies waiting.'

'Is it your girl-friend, Oom Alexander?' asked Marineka, and Beth found herself listening anxiously for the answer.

'Well, not *the* girl-friend, poppet, but she will do very nicely for this evening.'

'Is she pretty?'

'Oh, very…' he sounded absentminded as he paid the bill.

'Pretty clothes?' persisted his niece.

'Fabulous—and something different every time I

see her.' He looked across to Beth and smiled a little. 'Ready? Shall we get this lot home?'

The children were tired; they ate their suppers after a rowdy game of Happy Families and were got without difficulty to their beds. Beth, a little battered after supervising four baths and coaxing each of them to close their eyes and go to sleep, was quite tired herself. She wandered to her room and tidied herself, then, after a peep at her charges, went downstairs. She should be feeling on top of the world she told herself a little peevishly, living in super comfort in a wonderful house with absolutely nothing to do but keep an eye on the children, and yet here she was feeling sorry for herself because the evening stretched before her with nothing to do but eat Mrs Silver's delicious dinner and read or watch TV.

She went into the sitting room and sat down with a magazine; it was still too early for dinner and there were plenty of *Harpers* and *Vogues* lying around. She was intent on the latest fashions, when the professor came in—in a dinner jacket again, so he would be going somewhere rather splendid; the girl-friend, if Marineka was to be believed, would be the kind of girl who expected—and got—only VIP treatment. When he said: 'Hullo, Elizabeth. How about a sherry before I go?' it was surprising how all at once her world became fun, but he didn't sit down, only perched on the arm of a chair, talking about the children, telling her that their mother was making good progress, commenting on their afternoon in a casually friendly manner until he looked at his watch and put down his glass.

'I must go,' he told her, 'although I would much rather be staying quietly here and dining with you.' And when he saw her face: 'You don't believe me, do you? When you know me better you will find that I am not given to making impulsive remarks, although I daresay that if my deeper feelings were involved it might be otherwise. You're a very restful person, Elizabeth, as well as being a good and intelligent listener.'

She considered him thoughtfully. 'I should have thought after a busy week in theatre you would enjoy relaxing in the company of some pretty girl who hadn't the least idea what a kidney transplant was and didn't care either.'

He had strolled to the door. 'I'm taking the children to see their mother tomorrow morning,' was all he said. 'Please feel free to do exactly what you like until lunch-time. Good night, my dear Miss Partridge.'

She sat staring at the door, closing soundlessly behind him. A snub, even if a gentle one; she must have annoyed him in some way. Probably he considered that she had been too familiar—after all, his private life was nothing to do with her and men were prone to fits of uppishness; besides, she kept forgetting the fact that he was a consultant, an important one, and from the appearance of his house, a wealthy one at that; they had little in common, only their work. She really would have to try and remember that he had employed her as a nanny and do her best to behave like one.

She wasn't quite sure what he expected of her the next morning; she got up with the children and saw to their breakfasts, then when he came into the dining room, excused herself on the plea of getting their outdoor things ready and went upstairs, to be followed very shortly by Alberdina, stumping along on her short legs and demanding to wear her best coat, and the other three followed her shortly afterwards. Beth sent them all downstairs presently, ready to go out, clutching the variety of gifts they had for their mother, and when the front door shut behind them she went back to her room where she stood looking rather aimlessly out of the window.

It was a splendid morning again and to stay indoors was unthinkable; the vague idea of going back to the flat and getting a meal for William—doing his washing, perhaps, took shape in her head and became a certainty. She put on her jacket, found her handbag and gloves, ran down to the kitchen to tell Mrs Silver where she was going, and slipped out of the house. It was quiet in the Sunday streets and she had to wait a little while for a bus, but when it did arrive it was almost empty, so that it rattled along without any of the tiresome stops which plagued a weekday traveller. It was still early as she unlocked the flat door, and a good thing it was, she told herself ruefully, looking round at William's hopeless attempts at housekeeping. She took off her jacket, found a pinny, and got to work, only pausing for a cup of coffee after she had done the washing, Hoovered and dusted and made his bed.

A meal was the next thing; she made a shepherd's pie with a tin of corned beef, opened a tin of fruit, laid the table, left a brief note, and with one last look around, left the flat. It was barely twelve o'clock and there was plenty of time to get back to the professor's house and resume her guardianship of the children at lunch-time.

Mrs Silver answered the doorbell, ushering her in with a gentle flow of inconsequential chatter which took them across the hall to the foot of the staircase, where they were interrupted by Dirk, coming out of the sitting room. 'Uncle Alexander says will you please come in here,' he asked her, and as she followed him, shattered at having mistimed her morning so badly: 'Have you been out? We've been back ages—we're playing Scrabble.'

She looked guiltily across the room to where the professor was lying on the handsome carpet, his chin propped on a hand, frowning over the game.

'I'm so sorry,' she began. 'I didn't know you would be back so early—you said the morning, and I foolishly supposed...'

'Forgive me getting up, Elizabeth, and you haven't

been in the least foolish; I did indeed say until lunch-time, and I meant it. You have, in fact, almost an hour in which to do as you wish, but if you can bear to join us, we shall be delighted, although I should warn you that I shall be out for the rest of the day, so if you wish to savour the last of your freedom, we shall quite understand. Lunch is at a quarter past one.'

She laughed then and the children laughed with her. 'I love Scrabble,' she declared, and got down on her knees opposite the professor.

'You have been out?' he queried gently.

'Well, yes. I popped back to the flat.'

'William is a lucky fellow,' he murmured. 'I daresay you made his bed, cleaned the place from attic to cellar and cooked his dinner.'

It was her turn, so she didn't answer him at once. 'I like doing it,' she told him matter-of-factly, and knew that that wasn't quite true; she liked doing it up to a certain point, but just now and again she longed never to see the dingy little place again; to live in a gracious house like the one she was in at the present moment; to go shopping and buy whatever she wanted with money she hadn't spent months saving. 'It's your turn,' she warned him.

Beth didn't see the professor for the rest of the day, indeed, she didn't see him until the Monday evening. She had got the children to bed after what she was bound to admit had been a highly successful day, for they had been good; true, they had bickered and quarrelled, but only in the normal way of brothers and sisters, but they had done anything she had asked of them and eaten their meals without too much fuss. She had done her best to keep them occupied for as much of the day as possible and it seemed she had succeeded, for now they were in bed nicely tired. She was nicely tired too. She ate her solitary dinner and wondered about the professor; he would have had a ward teaching round that morning and probably a lecture as well, but the theatre list hadn't been too bad, she had seen it before she had left on the Friday, although in all probability it had bulged with emergencies before the end of the day.

Perhaps he wasn't coming home; he might have gone out again with the girl who was so well dressed and always wore different clothes each time he saw her. Beth admitted to a dislike of the unknown charmer, a thought which naturally enough led her to get up and study herself in the gilt framed mirror between the windows of the sitting room, with the futile wish that she could have been beautiful—a wish which brought her no comfort at all. She was turning her back on her unsatisfactory reflection when the professor walked in and she forgot her own small vexations at once; he looked tired, and his craggy, handsome face was haggard.

'You've had a bad day,' she said at once. 'What

happened? There wasn't a transplant this morning...'
Her beautiful eyes searched his, she looked and
sounded like an anxious, loving wife, and a tiny flicker
of tender amusement came and went in his eyes
although he answered seriously enough:

'The girl—remember her? She had a bad setback
this morning; luckily we were all there and able to deal
with it at once, but it took the greater part of the day.'

'She'll be all right?'

'I hope so; she's on sunflower seed oil, as you know,
and we're pretty sure it isn't a reject, more likely an
infection. With luck she'll pull through.'

'You've had no dinner?' and when he shook his
head, 'And no lunch either, I'll be bound. Shall I ask
Mrs Silver to get something for you?'

'She heard my key in the door and rushed away to
get something ready. Will you come and sit with me
while I eat, Elizabeth?'

She went with him into the dining room; of course
he would want to tell her about the case; she had
learned to listen to William a long time ago. He had
told her once that she was a good listener because she
didn't interrupt or ask silly questions and understood
what he was talking about; she hoped the professor
would find her all of those things.

Mrs Silver must have moved like lightning, for
the table was already laid. The professor went over
to a side table and poured himself a whisky and

turned to Beth. 'You'll have a glass of sherry, or do you prefer Madeira?'

She hadn't had that since she had lived at home; she accepted a glass and went to sit in a crinoline chair beside the vast sideboard, but when Mrs Silver returned with a tray and set a plate of soup before the professor he begged her to join him at the table, so she took the chair beside his and listened quietly while he told her about his day. He had finished his soup, the delicious Sole Mornay which followed it, and eaten most of one of Mrs Silver's fruit tarts before he had told her everything, and because he wanted to explain a particular underwater drainage he had decided upon, he pushed his plate to one side and started drawing diagrams on the back of an envelope. And Beth listened carefully and studied his drawings closely; it was more than likely that sooner or later she would need to know all about it. She was studying his diagrams closely when she was startled to hear him say: 'You really are a dear girl; here have I been boring on and you haven't yawned once.'

She looked up to smile at him. 'Why should I yawn? I'm interested—it's my work too, you know, in a lesser degree.'

He nodded. 'You plan to stay in hospital? You have no thought of marrying?'

She grinned engagingly. 'No thought at all. You

see, I'm not very well endowed. A plain girl with some money might get married, but a plain girl without any doesn't stand much of a chance. If I were pretty it would be easy enough to get married. Men,' state Beth seriously, 'like pretty girls.'

He was peeling a peach, now he put it on a plate and handed it to her and began one for himself. 'Of course men like pretty girls; it would be a strange world if we didn't.' He smiled suddenly. 'The children think you're pretty, did you know that?'

'No—and how nice of you to tell me; people usually keep nice things to themselves and pass on the nasty remarks.'

'You sound bitter, dear girl.' He leaned back in his chair, studying her quite openly. 'Tell me about yourself,' he invited.

'There's nothing to tell.' She spoke too quickly and he said softly:

'Ah, I see that I must wait. What does William intend to do at the end of the year?'

It was easy enough to talk about William. 'He's going to try for a surgical job—somewhere where he'll get plenty of experience—the Midlands.'

'You will go with him?'

'Me? No. He'll live in wherever he is; besides, he'll be moving around until he feels he can try for a regis-trar's post and his Fellowship.'

'And you will stay at St Elmer's?'

'Well, yes...' She saw her future in her mind's eye and didn't much care for it. She added rather crossly, 'What else should I do?'

'I can think of a number of things. Shall we have coffee in the sitting room?'

She poured their coffee from the little silver Queen Anne coffee pot into Spode china cups and passed him the sugar. The curtains were drawn now and the room looked, despite its magnificence, delightfully home-like. She cast a lingering look around her and caught her companion's eye.

'This is a lovely house, and when one is in it, one forgets that London is just outside.'

He agreed gravely. 'And yet I prefer the country, as I believe you do. Do you ride, Elizabeth?'

'Yes—at least, I used to. We had a pony when we were children, and then there was Beauty...my step-brother wanted to sell them after my father's death, but we persuaded him not to. They'll be old now—I hope they're well cared for.'

'Why not?—perhaps they are out to graze at some farm.'

'There were some people called Truscott—they had a farm near Chifney, they may have taken them...'

'What did you call the pony?' His voice was placid and she glanced at him; he didn't look tired now; he was unwinding.

'Sugar—he loved it. If Truscotts took them they

wouldn't be far away—they were at the other end of the village.'

'Ah—Chifney.'

Beth shook her head. 'No, that's my home, the village is Langton Magna.'

'A small village with a long name, I take it?'

'That's right, it's very pretty there.'

'The English countryside is delightful—tell me about it, Elizabeth.'

She liked the way he called her Elizabeth; she would have to be careful when she got back to St Elmer's, though; it would never do to be on such a free and easy footing with him there. It was surprising to her that although they had known each other for such a short time, she should feel so easy with him, as though she had known him all her life—and he would be going back to Holland very soon and she would never see him again. But in the meantime she would tell him about Chifney and the village because he seemed to be enjoying it, though probably he wouldn't remember any of it once he was away from England. She said now, a little hesitantly:

'Well, if you would really like to know...' and told him about the house and the village and the people who lived there, although she told him nothing about herself; she had, she remembered uneasily, already told him too much before, although it wasn't likely that he remembered much of it. He didn't appear to be paying much attention to her now and she kept her chatter deliberately light and after a little while declared her intention of going to bed; it disappointed her a little that he made no attempt to persuade her to remain with him a little longer.

He showed little wish to share her company during the next few days either; they met at occasional meals, or passing each other in the hall on their way in or out, but usually the children were with her, and if he had any time to spare he gave it to his small relations. Beth felt that she was beginning to turn into a real live governess and that it was a good thing that within a day or so she would be back in the Recovery Room, so she was all the more surprised when at breakfast on Friday morning he asked her to accompany him to hospital. 'I haven't a list this afternoon,' he explained, 'and Martina wants to see you.'

She buttered toast. 'What about the children?'

'Mrs Silver has promised to look after them until we get back. I should like you to come, Miss Partridge.'

She was tempted to think of some excuse because he looked so sure that he would get his own way, but he had spoken in the same terms that he might have used if he had been asking her to put up a drip or alter the flow of the oxygen, so she said: 'Very well, Professor,' and busied herself cutting Alberdina's toast into fingers.

She was glad that she was already wearing the

tweed suit, although she didn't feel that it really did justice to her companion's elegance as she joined him in the hall, but her hair had gone up perfectly that morning with no stray ends, and all the outdoor exercise she had had with the children had pinkened her cheeks in a most attractive manner. She smoothed her leather gloves over her capable hands and sat quietly beside him while he manoeuvred the car through the traffic. She was neither ill-mannered nor particularly shy, but after a quick glance at his face, it seemed to her that to chatter nothings while he had such a preoccupied look on his face wouldn't have done at all; it was only when he stopped outside the hospital's main entrance that she asked: 'Shall I go up to the ward? I expect you have things to do...'

He stared at her from beneath his hooded lids. 'No, I have nothing to do, we will go together.'

He disdained the lift; by skipping up the stairs without pause Beth was able to keep pace with him, but only just. At the top of the first flight she said tartly, 'There are two more flights of stairs, if you don't slow down I shall just stay where I am.'

He stopped at once. 'My dear girl, I'm sorry. I was thinking.'

'Yes, I know. Is something worrying you?'

He was leaning against the hideous wrought iron balustrade. 'Hardly that—ask me again in ten minutes or so and I'll tell you.'

They went on up, at a more sober pace now, until they reached the Private Patients' Wing, where, after a brief pause in Sister's office, they went along to Mevrouw Thorbecke's room. She was up, sitting by the window in the most gorgeous dressing gown Beth had ever seen, and surrounded by flowers. She smiled as they went in, offering her brother a cheek to kiss and gave a hand to Beth as she said in a friendly voice:

'I hear from my brother that you have been wonderful with the children, and I am so grateful. Will you sit down? Has he told you about his—our plan?'

'No.' Beth turned to look at the professor, lounging on the end of the bed, his hands in his pockets, apparently not very interested in the conversation.

'We—that is I—would be so happy if you would come with me and the children into the country, just for—shall we say two weeks? I know that it must seem impossible to you, but it can be arranged. The children are so fond of you and although I am almost well I do not think that I could manage without help.' She paused and Beth took the opportunity to say: 'It's very kind of you to want me, Mevrouw Thorbecke, but I haven't any more holiday to spare...'

'Not holiday, it seems that you can be lent. I do not understand it at all, but Alexander knows all about it.' She looked anxiously at Beth. 'You do not perhaps like the idea of spending two more weeks with the children?'

'Well, I hadn't thought about it,' said Beth with

truth. 'I like them and I've enjoyed this week very much, but I don't want to lose my job.'

The professor spoke at last. 'There is no fear of that, I will guarantee that you return to St Elmer's the moment you wish to. I've already spoken to all the necessary people—it's for you to decide; you have only to say that you would prefer not to go with my sister.'

'How long exactly would you want me to stay? I have to think about William.'

'Ah, yes—William. Do you suppose he could manage for another couple of weeks?' He got off the bed and came over to her chair. 'Dear girl,' he said quietly, 'will you do this for me?'

Something in his voice made her look at him; his expression was as placid as usual, but his eyes were curiously intent. She told herself that she was being a weak-minded fool as she heard herself agreeing to go.

CHAPTER FOUR

LATER after the professor had taken her back to the house and gone again, Beth wondered what on earth had possessed her to agree to his wishes; she liked the children, and she had enjoyed the week at his house, but there were several reasons why it might not be convenient now that she had had time for reflection. The flat and William, for instance—who would clean the former and look after the latter? A little belatedly she wished she had asked for time to see William before she had consented go to away for a further two weeks. She thought about it, on and off, for the rest of the day, so that the children accused her of being absentminded more than once, and when Professor van Zeust came home at last after tea, she waylaid him on his way to his study. 'Could you spare me a few minutes, Professor?' she wanted to know.

He stopped to stare at her. 'Second thoughts, Elizabeth?' He smiled a little. 'Yes, of course you may have as many minutes as you want—come in.'

He waved her to a chair by the window and sat himself on the edge of his desk. 'Well?' he inquired.

She wasn't a girl to beat about the bush. 'I should like time to see William; I should have talked to him before I agreed to go with Mevrouw Thorbecke—I can't think why I didn't think of it then.'

'This evening?' His instant agreement took her by surprise. 'Why not? It is something I should have thought of, too. Is he off duty or shall we go to the hospital?'

'He's on call for Cas.'

'In that case we'll go when the children have been put to bed, and ask Mrs Silver to put back dinner until we return.'

Beth raised her pansy eyes to his. 'Oh, but there's no need for you to take me. I'll jump on a bus.'

'You will come with me in the car.' He sounded quite definite about it, and then, smiling his charming smile, 'And I promise you that if you want to change your mind there will be no hard feelings.'

'Thank you, and I'm sorry to be such a nuisance, but I don't think I could go until I've seen William.'

'Of course not.' He got off the desk and walked round to the chair behind it; very likely he had work to do, so Beth thanked him again and went back to the children, feeling considerably relieved at his readiness to fall in with her ideas. Her relief might not have been so profound if she had overheard the conversation he had on the telephone as soon as she was safely out of earshot.

They left a couple of hours later, the children safely tucked up for the night, and the professor, while his usual friendly self, made no mention of the matter uppermost in her mind. At the hospital entrance he declared that he had something to discuss with the Senior Registrar, and left her to make her way to Casualty, on the chance of finding William there. He was, sitting in Sister's office with Staff Nurse King, drinking tea; the place empty of patients and having that brooding silence such places always have once everyone has gone home for the day; that it would fill up presently was a certainty; it always did, but now it was peaceful enough in an uneasy kind of way and she could see that William was in a good mood. She nodded to Harriet King, with whom she was friendly enough in a vague way, and asked if she might have a word with her brother.

'Only a minute or two, William—I'm glad I caught you before the evening rush.'

Harriet got up. 'Go ahead,' she invited. 'I've got those wretched lists to fetch from the office—I'll go now.' She paused on her way out. 'Help yourself to tea, ducky.'

It surprised Beth that William didn't want to know why she had come, indeed, she had the impression that he had been expecting her, which was absurd, but he was an easy-going young man and always had been; she wasted no time on speculation but said at once: 'Mevrouw Thorbecke wants me to go back home with her and the children for another two weeks—somewhere in the country.' She paused, realizing that she had forgotten to ask where exactly it was. 'I said I'd go and then afterwards I thought you might not be able to manage on your own.'

He grinned at her. 'Don't worry about me, Beth—funnily enough, Dobson'—Dobson was a new house surgeon, a quiet retiring young man she had met several times—'asked me only this morning if I knew of anywhere where he could live for a couple of weeks—he took over from Bill Knight, you know, but can't go into his room because Bill's got some virus or other, so poor old Dobson's been living at a bed and breakfast place and hating it. He could move in with me for those two weeks and share the rent and so on—that should suit us all.'

'Well, I don't know—will you be able to manage?'

'Oh, don't worry about it, love. We'll get that old soul in the basement to come up and clean the place and do most of our eating in the hospital—of course we'll manage. I'll give him a ring now, if you like.'

It wasn't a bad idea, in fact it was wonderfully convenient. It was more than likely that the place would be in a frightful state when she got back, but William would have company, and over and above that, two more weeks at the princely salary she was receiving would mean more than a pair of shoes for William—he would be able to have a good deal more than that, and so would she. 'OK,' she said finally, and listened while he talked into the telephone. When he put it down he said cheerfully: 'Dobson's no end pleased, he'll move in when I give the word. Will you be coming back to the flat before you leave?'

This was something else she hadn't thought about; really, the professor had given her no time to consider anything. 'I don't know, but I'll have to ask for some time off—I'll need some more clothes.'

'Well, let me know. I'll...' He was interrupted by the sing-song wail of the ambulance, approaching fast. 'Ah, the evening session—be seeing you, Beth.'

She went through the department and out the other end, so as to avoid the patient's arrival; it meant trailing through Outpatients to reach the hospital entrance through a long, dreary passage, seldom used once OPD had closed down for the night; it had hard wooden benches set at intervals, to take the overflow from the various clinics, each one in an alcove between the row of tall narrow windows. It was getting towards dusk by now and no one had switched on the lights; to anyone strange to St Elmer's, it might have presented a somewhat cheerless aspect, but Beth took no notice of it; she knew every inch of it by heart and could have walked it blindfold. She was half-way along it when her eye fell on someone sitting on one of the benches. It lay in shadow and until she went closer she was unable to see whether it was a man or a woman. It was a girl, quite young—fifteen or sixteen, she supposed, huddled up and greenish white, her eyes closed.

Beth bent over her, feeling her pulse, which was far too rapid, then spoke to her gently. It was a few seconds before the girl opened her eyes. 'I gotta pain,' she said dully.

'Yes, dear—could you tell me where it is?'

'Me stomach.'

The girl was terribly pale, so pale that Beth cast a searching eye around her; patients with stab wounds looked like that, so did ruptured ulcers, only that wasn't likely to be the case here. 'Have you had an accident?' she asked.

'No—just got this pain—proper awful it is too.'

'I'm going to find a doctor. Will you stay here? I'll only be a minute or so. Did you think this was Casualty?'

The girl gave her a dull stare. 'Came 'ere ter sit down. Don't be long, will yer?' And she added in a frightened whisper: 'I think I'm goin' ter die.'

'No, you're not. I'm a nurse even though I'm not in uniform.' Beth gave her a reassuring pat and with a last injunction to sit quiet until she got back, hurried away. It was quicker to go straight to the entrance hall now; the porter could get a doctor and a stretcher at the same time. She burst into it now and the first person she saw was the professor, standing idly by the entrance. He turned as she reached his side and began without preliminary: 'There's a girl—' her voice was urgent but not panicky. 'She's sitting in the corridor behind OPD. She's pallid and in great pain—abdominal, her pulse is rapid and weak. She says she hasn't had an accident and I couldn't see any signs of a wound.'

He took her hand and said in a calm voice, 'We'll take a look, shall we? Which way?'

The girl was still there, moaning now; when she saw them she whispered: 'Pain's awful—is this the doc?'

Beth nodded and flew to turn on the lights, bleak glass-shaded pendants which allowed them a better sight of the girl. The professor was already bending over her and said almost immediately: 'Get porters and a trolley, Beth—tell Hill to get Professor MacDonald's registrar—he's on the surgical side. I've just been there with him—ask him to go to Casualty.'

She wasted no time and when she got back from giving her messages the porters were already there, about to wheel the girl into Casualty.

She went too, not quite knowing what to do, and it was a good thing that she did; Harriet King had her hands full with a road accident and William was scrubbing up at one of the sinks. The professor took in the situation at a glance; he murmured briefly to William and then looked over his shoulder at Beth. 'Perhaps we could manage until Staff Nurse is free?' he suggested. 'If you would get some clothes off her and find out her name and address.'

He turned back to William and Beth told the porters

to put the trolley in one of the curtained cubicles and began to get her patient undressed. A difficult job; the girl was in great pain and never still, but even more difficult was the task of finding out her name and where she lived. She was ready for examination, wrapped carefully in a blanket, before Beth was able to discover that she was Tracey Blake and that she lived at number twenty, Melscham Road, one of the dingy streets only a few minutes from the hospital. 'I feel awful,' she muttered as Beth put her head round the curtains to say that she was ready and then went back to hold the girl's cold hand.

The registrar had arrived by now and had joined the professor in his examination of the patient. The two men were very gentle as well as thorough; at length the professor straightened his back and looked across to his colleague. 'It's an ectopic—a classical example of internal bleeding, pallor, severe pain.' He raised his eyebrows in mute inquiry and added: 'Straight away, don't you think? We'll have to have a cross-match— theatre in fifteen minutes? Could you arrange it?'

The registrar hurried away and the professor turned to the girl. 'Tracey, we can get rid of that pain for you, but we shall have to operate in just a short time. You won't know anything about it and when it's all over and you wake up, the pain will be gone.'

'Promise?'

'Oh, yes, I promise. How old are you?'

'Fifteen.'

He glanced round to where Beth was standing. 'Miss Partridge, get the Path Lab here for a cross-match, will you, and tell Hill to get whichever anaesthetist is on call, and someone must contact her parents so that we can have a consent form.'

'I'll go,' said Beth. 'I know where she lives and it's close by, I can be back in ten minutes. I'll give your messages to Hill on the way out.'

She hurried through the drab streets, wondering as she went why the professor called her Beth at one moment and Miss Partridge at the next; she could think of no satisfactory answer, though, and there was really no time... She found number twenty without difficulty and banged on its shabby door. The woman who answered it didn't look too friendly, but then, Beth acknowledged silently, if she lived in a place like Melscham Road, she wouldn't be all that forthcoming to strangers herself. She asked in her pleasant voice: 'Mrs Blake? You have a daughter called Tracey?'

The woman stared at her. 'S'right.'

'Well, I'm sorry to tell you that she's at St Elmer's; she came to get help for a pain and she requires an urgent operation. Would you come back with me and sign a consent form?'

The woman showed neither surprise nor distress. 'Now wot's she bin up to?' she demanded. 'Perfect little 'orror that girl's bin, always on the streets. I can't come.'

'Then your husband? It will only take a few minutes.'

'E's in the pub, yer won't get 'im ter go.'

Beth paused; they had been joined by the neighbours living on either side, listening unashamedly and with great interest. 'Tracey ill, is she?' cried one of them. 'Wot's she got?'

Beth sensed an ally. 'Something wrong inside, it's urgent...'

'Yer got ter go,' urged the second woman, 'praps she'll die and then where'll yer be? Up before the beak, most likely—lot o' nosey parkers. You go along, Mrs. Blake. I'll keep an eye on young Bert and Elsie.'

She cast an inquiring eye over Beth. 'And 'oo are you?' she wanted to know.

'A Staff nurse at St Elmer's—there wasn't time to ring the police and get them to bring a message.'

'There yer are—you get a move on, Mrs Blake, like I said, and one of us'll slip across ter the Swan and tell yer 'usband.'

'Oh, well,' Mrs Blake agreed reluctantly, and with still more reluctance fetched a shapeless cardigan and a terrible felt hat which she crammed on to her untidy head without recourse to a mirror. 'I 'ope it's worth it,' she told Beth darkly as she joined her.

Tracey was still in Casualty with Harriet King, being got ready for theatre, and there was no sign of either the professor or the registrar, or even William, a state of affairs which didn't please Mrs Blake at all.

She took one look at her daughter, wanted to know impatiently what she'd been up to, and demanded to see a doctor, and Beth, who had been filling out the consent form for her to sign and listening with one ear to Emily's efforts to explain that the Casualty Officer would return in a very short time, picked up the telephone and asked Hill to fetch Professor van Zeust or his registrar down at once.

The professor came, walking without undue haste, looking calm and a little grave, just, thought Beth approvingly, exactly how a professor of surgery should look. Mrs Blake must have shared the same thought, for she stopped her complaining at once and waited for him to speak.

'Mrs Blake? I am glad that you came so promptly, I am only sorry if this has been a shock to you. Tracey needs an immediate abdominal operation, I'm afraid, but of course we can do nothing until you or her father will consent to it.'

'Wot's up with 'er?' asked Mrs Blake, and added uncertainly, 'Doc.'

'She is bleeding severely inside; she had already lost a good deal of blood and we cannot afford to wait, but I am confident that we can put matters right if we see to it now.'

'OK. But mind you, Doc, I want ter know all about it. Is it a baby?'

He looked at her gravely. 'Something of that sort. If you will wait here I will come and talk to you about it as soon as I have operated.'

"Ow long's that?"

His calm was unruffled. 'An hour. You will be able to see her when she goes to the ward.'

'Oh—so I 'as ter wait 'ere, I suppose?'

His eyes flickered towards Beth. 'Please, and I am sure that Staff Nurse will keep you company and get you some tea. You have signed the form?'

He went away without another glance at Beth, who supposed that he had forgotten that she wasn't on duty, nor in uniform, nor, for that matter, had anything to do with the affair; she had found the girl, it was true, but she had handed her over to the right people and should have been allowed to disappear quietly about her own business. Oh, well, she thought resignedly, she had had nothing to do that evening, anyway.

The hour passed very slowly. Mrs Blake, drinking one cup of tea after another, and smoking cigarettes non-stop, spoke very little. Beth, under the mistaken impression that she was upset about her daughter, tried several lines of cheerful sympathetic talk without much result; it wasn't until she had ploughed her way through half an hour of this kind of comfort that Mrs Blake horrified her by saying: 'Don't come the soft chat with me, ducks, our Tracey 'asn't bin 'ome for weeks—always was a little nuisance, I can tell yer.

There ain't no love lost between us, I can tell yer and 'er dad don't bother with 'er, neither.'

This forthright statement had the effect of drying up Beth completely; she fetched another cup of tea and was profoundly relieved when the professor joined them.

'I'm sorry you have had to wait,' he told Mrs Blake, 'but if we might have that little talk about Tracey...?' He paused and Beth rightly interpreted the pause as a hint for her to make herself scarce. As she reached the door he called out to her: 'Get Hill to telephone home and tell Mrs Silver, will you? About half an hour.'

She gave the message and then wandered about the empty grandeur of the entrance hall. She didn't like to go to Cas. to see if William was there; besides, if he was, he would be busy and she wouldn't be able to talk to him, and if he wasn't there, she hadn't the least idea where he might be. She paced round and round, wanting her dinner, wanting to get away from the hospital and the chain smoking, unfeeling Mrs Blake; it was frightening to know that there were mothers like her, and still more frightening wondering what would happen to Tracey. Her head began to ache and she went and leaned her forehead on the glass of the door to cool it.

'Ah, there you are,' said the professor cheerfully, coming up behind her at such a great rate that she had no time to turn round, but was swept through the doors without further ado and into the car, and was being driven away before she could ask: 'She's all right? She'll pull through?'

'Yes—we caught her just in time—thanks to you, dear girl.' His voice was warm, but she sensed that he didn't want to talk just then, so she sat silent as he drove through the thinly trafficked streets, and when they reached his house and he got out to open its door for her, she went in quickly and made for the stairs; possibly he had a great deal on his mind and didn't want company, and if he didn't mention dinner she would say nothing either, but go to the kitchen later and get Mrs Silver to give her something on a tray.

But she had barely taken a step when she was stopped by his hand clamped on to a shoulder, and twiddled round to face him. 'Beth, what should I have done without you this evening? So quick and sensible and kind.' He bent suddenly and kissed her. 'You are a gem of a girl.'

The wholly delightful sensation this engendered in her was shattered by his careless: 'Lord, I'm famished, aren't you? I wonder what Mrs Silver has for us?'

Whatever it was, she found that she had no appetite for it; she wasn't a girl who had been kissed all that much, but when she was, she preferred to be kissed with due deliberation, not in the same breath as an urgent demand for dinner. She stifled peevishness as she sat down to table with him, and in the intervals of not doing justice to Mrs Silver's delicious cooking,

asked him the sort of questions she imagined he
wished to be asked. He answered them readily enough,
even going to great lengths to tell her the future Tracey
had so nearly lost would be restored to her with the
help of the social worker.

'I had no idea that you were so immersed in your
work,' he commented dryly as they sat over their
coffee, and she was on the point of telling him that she
wasn't, really, only she had wanted to know about
poor little Tracey, when it occurred to her that he was
really only making conversation; his thoughts were
far away with something—or someone—else. She
lapsed into silence until he asked: 'You saw William,
I suppose? Everything is arranged, I hope?'

'Yes, thank you.' She would have told him more
about that, but the idea had taken root that he was
becoming bored with her; as long as things had been
arranged satisfactorily to suit his sister, he wasn't interested further. She swallowed the rest of her coffee and
excused herself on the plea of having letters to write
before she went to bed. He went to open the door for
her with the easy good manners which she found so
pleasant, and wished her good night in a voice which,
while friendly, held none of the tones which she had
heard—or imagined she had heard?—earlier that
evening. Something had put him out, she thought as
she went upstairs, or else he was worried. She fell into
uneasy sleep, trying to decide which it was.

Viewed in the cheerful brightness of an early morning in April, though, she had to admit to herself that her mood of the previous evening had been a silly one. What had she to brood about, anyway? The professor had every right to be thoughtful or annoyed if he wished, and if he had felt like kissing her as a mark of appreciation for her help, there was no need for her to enlarge upon that, either. She jumped out of bed, telling herself robustly not to waste time worrying about things which were really none of her business.

Mevrouw Thorbecke came home two days later, looking a little pale and tired. The professor had driven her back himself, and Beth, who had hardly set eyes on him during the last couple of days, greeted him politely as he helped his sister into the house before suggesting to the invalid that bed might be welcome after the exertions of leaving hospital. 'The children are dying to see you,' she explained, 'and I thought it would be far less tiring for you if I were to pop you into bed first.' An idea to which the professor subscribed wholeheartedly, so that Mevrouw Thorbecke was assisted upstairs to her room and made comfortable before the children were allowed to visit her; a prudent move as it turned out, for they were wild with excitement, all wanting to talk at once, so that Beth's tactful suggestion that they should eat their supper while their mother had a light meal herself, sitting comfortably in bed, was welcomed by the invalid, even though the routine of the household was a little put out.

'But there,' said Mrs Silver, a good deal later, serving Beth's solitary dinner in the dining room, 'it makes no odds, does it, miss? With the professor out all the evening and Mevrouw nicely settled in, and all those dear children tucked up for the night. You'll be glad to get to your own bed, I don't doubt. A tiring day it's been.'

Beth agreed; it had been busy enough, true, although she wasn't tired, indeed she would have welcomed some company in which to eat her dinner, although she quite saw that the professor was hardly likely to stay home in order to entertain her. She praised Mrs Silver's cooking, helped to clear the table because it was Miss Powers' half day off and then went to cast an eye over her various charges. The children were asleep, their faces angelic in the dim night lights; their mother was sitting up in bed leafing through a magazine which she put down as Beth entered.

'What a dear girl you are,' she exclaimed warmly. 'Alexander told me that you were a treasure, and he is quite right. Are the children asleep?' And when Beth reassured her that they were: 'Would you be a dear and rearrange my pillows? I believe I shall go to sleep too, it is so nice to be back in this room. Must I take a sleeping tablet?'

'Not if you feel sleepy; look, see how you get on

while I have a bath and get ready for bed and when I'm ready I'll come back, if you're still awake I'll give you something. Is there anything you need for the night?'

Beth cast a long look round the luxurious room. It had, as far as she could see, just everything anyone could possibly need. 'I'll be back presently.'

It was still quite early, only a little after nine o'clock. She took her time over her bath and then, as the grandfather clock on the landing chimed its gentle hour, pottered along to see how Mevrouw Thorbecke was faring. The house was quiet, Mrs Silver was somewhere below, the maid wouldn't be back yet and there had been no sign of the professor. The landing was dimly lit and in the great oval mirror opposite the clock she could see her reflection, blue-dressing-gowned, her hair swinging in a bronze plaited rope; she didn't look too bad in the half dark, she thought, and giggled softly.

Mevrouw Thorbecke was asleep, looking like an older edition of her children; there would be no need of sleeping tablets—Beth turned out all but one of the lamps and went back the way she had come, to halt suddenly half-way across the landing, because the professor was coming upstairs two at a time and had already seen her.

'Hullo,' he greeted her in a loud whisper, and then: 'You look nice like that.'

'It's the dim light,' she answered composedly, 'you can't see me properly.' She added briskly: 'Mevrouw Thorbecke's asleep—and the children.'

'Splendid. I'm sorry that I had to go out this evening, there was no avoiding it—a date made some time ago.'

Who with? she wondered while she stated in a placid voice that it hadn't mattered at all; the children had been so happy to have their mother home again. She stopped in some confusion because that had sounded as though they hadn't been happy while she had been in hospital. 'Not that they weren't perfectly content with you,' she added fairly.

'And you? Have you been happy with me too?'

She looked at him cautiously, not sure if he were joking; he had probably had a simply splendid evening and was feeling on top of his world. She said in a colourless voice: 'I have been very happy here, thank you, Professor. The children are charming...'

They had been standing at the top of the staircase; she was quite unprepared when he caught her by the hand and hurried her down it. At the bottom, before she could say anything, he told her: 'Mrs Silver's making me some coffee—have a cup with me, Beth? I haven't had time to talk over our plans with you.'

She accompanied him into the study and sat down on a rather stiff chair, looking, despite her plait of hair and dressing-gown, just as though she were standing before one of the surgeons, taking instructions for the next case, and perhaps the professor thought so too, for there was a little smile twitching the corners of his mouth as he sat down at his desk. All the same he spoke seriously enough.

'There are no complications with Martina; she is bound to feel tired and perhaps depressed, but not for long. I thought that you might all go down to Somerset in a couple of days' time—will that suit you?' He hardly waited for her nod. 'You must, of course, have some time to see to your own affairs—an afternoon perhaps—would that be sufficient?' Again she nodded. 'Good, that's settled, then. I'll arrange to be free so that I can run you all down.'

'You said Somerset,' said Beth. 'Which part?'

'Just outside Castle Cary.'

'But that's not far from Chifney...'

'So it is,' he was smiling a little.

'But I remember telling you about Chifney—you asked me—you never said that you'd been there.'

He looked at her blandly. 'But I haven't, my dear girl, I go to Kenton Mackerell so seldom.'

Several questions pertinent to this statement trembled on her lips, but she didn't allow herself to utter them, for it struck her that probably he hadn't even thought about it until she had mentioned it, and after all, Kenton Mackerell was fourteen miles from Shepton Mallett, the nearest town of any size to Chifney. She would, one day when she was free, go over and take a look at her old home, not to go in, of course, but just to see it from the outside. She sighed, and he asked at once: 'Tired? Here's the coffee and I've no doubt Mrs Silver has made some sandwiches.'

He was right, the tray was laden, and Beth, invited to share them, fell to with quite an appetite. Presently she sat back and said: 'That was super. Is there anything else you wanted to tell me, Professor?'

He put his cup down. 'Two weeks more, then—if you can bear with the children for that length of time?' He smiled. 'At the same salary, naturally, and as much free time as you can manage—I haven't spoken to Martina about that yet, but I daresay you will be able to work out something.'

She got to her feet. 'Of course. Could I have tomorrow afternoon free to pack my things, do you suppose?'

'Why not? Go after lunch and stay as long as you need to, I'm sure Mrs Silver will cope for a few hours. I'll tell Martina in the morning. Now go to bed, Beth.'

She felt herself dismissed, although kindly. She murmured good night and left him standing in the doorway, watching her as she went up the staircase, as quiet as a mouse. In her room she made haste into her bed, intending to meditate over the important question of what clothes to take with her and what she needed to do when she got to the flat, but instead of that, she lay and thought about the professor until sleep overcame her.

CHAPTER FIVE

THEY set out after breakfast in a heavy downpour of rain, with the professor driving the Citroën, his sister beside him and Beth and the children packed snugly in the back with Alberdina curled up on her lap.

The children chattered away happily, not caring about the weather, pouring out information about the house they were going to in an English which became steadily worse as they got more excited; only Dirk stayed calmer than the others. 'Ducks and geese,' he told Beth, 'and calves, and there are two big horses as well as a donkey—we did tell you, remember? Do you like the country, Beth?'

'Yes, very much.' Her voice was light although her thoughts, remembering Chifney, were sad. 'I was brought up in a small village, except while I was away at school.'

This remark triggered off a further excited babble of chatter which lasted until they stopped in Andover, where it was momentarily quenched by glasses of milk and sticky buns, while the grown-ups sat drinking their coffee and glad of ten minutes' peace. And when they went on again presently, the children, the first flush of excitement over, were a good deal quieter, so that Beth, as they neared their destination, had the leisure to look around at well-remembered landmarks.

She knew Castle Cary well enough; a pleasant bustling little town set in the quiet Somerset country-side. They went through it without stopping and once on its outskirts, turned down a narrow, tree-lined lane half-way down which wide gates stood open on to a pleasant, not too big garden surrounding a stone farm-house of a comfortable size. Smaller than Chifney, she saw at once, but perfectly maintained, with its mul-lioned windows and tall twisted chimneys, with a cluster of outbuildings at its back; it would be fun to explore, but that was for later. She shepherded the children out of the car, suggesting practically that if the professor would see his sister to her room, she would help her to bed. 'For it has been a long drive and a bit noisy, I'm afraid,' she observed with her usual good sense. 'An hour or two's rest after lunch in bed will do a world of good. I'll get the children indoors first.'

Mevrouw Thorbecke looked grateful and the pro-fessor agreed, saying:

'Mrs Burge should be here—ah, there she is. Hand the children over to her, Beth, and come upstairs with us.'

Mrs Burge was small and thin and instantly enveloped in the children's hugs, to emerge and greet Mevrouw Thorbecke and the professor and lastly Beth, whom she eyed a little doubtfully as she smiled and shook hands and wished her good day in a soft Somerset voice.

The hall was bright with flowers and sunlight, and there was a nice smell of baking coming from the kitchen. Beth glanced around her as she followed the others up the uncarpeted oak stairs. She supposed the house belonged to Mevrouw Thorbecke's husband, and from what the children had said, she gathered that they seldom came more than once a year, and yet the place showed no signs of having been closed for months on end; the furniture shone with polish, there was not a speck of dust to be seen and the carpet under her feet bore every sign of constant care. Perhaps Mrs Burge lived the whole year in the house, acting as caretaker as well as housekeeper.

In the long narrow corridor at the head of the stairs, she opened the door the professor indicated, into a room which reminded her strongly of Chifney—dark furniture and a bed whose chintz cover matched the curtains and chairs, and a silky carpet underfoot—a restful, sweet-smelling room, it would have been like that for generations; people living in the country weren't so prone to follow fashion slavishly, and if curtains and hangings had to be replaced they would, like as not, search far and wide to get exactly the same pattern as before.

The professor put down the case he was carrying, consigned his sister to her care and went downstairs again, where she could hear him urging the children to wash their hands for lunch.

Mevrouw Thorbecke was tired but cheerful enough. 'I feel a fraud, going to bed in this way,' she admitted, 'but I am weary, Beth. You are sure that you don't mind being left with the children for the rest of the day?'

'Not a bit,' said Beth stoutly. 'They can show me round and I daresay they'll go to bed willingly enough and sleep like tops if we spend the afternoon out of doors.' She settled the pillows just so behind her patient, and with the promise of lunch on a tray just as soon as it could be arranged, she went downstairs.

The car had gone from before the door and there was no sign of her luggage. She was on the point of going in search of it when the professor came round the side of the house. 'I'll take you to your room in a moment,' he promised. 'Mrs Burge is getting a tray ready for Martina and the children are upstairs. Come and have a drink.'

He swept her along with him into a large, low-ceilinged room, beamed and panelled and furnished with comfortable sofas and armchairs, and here again there was chintz and a thick carpet underfoot.

'I really should...' she began, 'the children...'

'Sherry first. Sit down, do.'

She sat, accepted her glass and sipped. The sherry

was good; she shut her eyes for a second, listening to the vague country sounds coming in through the open windows. London and their miserable little flat seemed very far away.

'I am going back this evening, after dinner.' The professor's voice, very quiet, merged nicely into her dreamy thoughts. 'What shall you do with the children, have you any idea?'

'Well, could they show me round? They seem to love the place very much and there's a lot to see, isn't there? And after tea we could make some plans, perhaps, there must be things they specially want to do while they're here. They should be tired enough by bedtime. Would you tell me what you would like me to do exactly? I mean, I know I look after the children and help Mevrouw Thorbecke once in a while, but is there anything else?'

'Good God, girl, that sounds like slave labour! Mrs Burge sees to the housekeeping and cooks and she has ample help; you'll not need to lift a finger. She has a niece who will take the children for a couple of hours when you want to be free; I'll leave you to see to that, and as for Martina, she needs nothing beyond companionship and a little reassurance. I think you will find that within a very short time she will want to join in the children's quiet activities. But not just yet—she is tired, isn't she? Do what you think fit, Beth; I'll leave you in charge. We will have lunch in a few minutes and go round the place; you're quite right, the children love it here, it is a pity that they only visit me once a year.'

She had finished her sherry and he took her glass from her and went over to the side table. 'I should like them to come more often, but my sister and brother-in-law have a pleasant home in Willemstad and they don't like leaving it too often.'

She stared at him in surprise. 'Oh, it's your house—I don't know why I thought it was Mevrouw Thorbecke's, at least, I assumed it was because you've already got one house in London.'

He looked meek. 'I'm afraid I own this one too—my godmother, you know. Perhaps I should have sold it, but I came here a great deal as a boy and I'm fond of it. I'm fond of the London house too.'

Beth coloured faintly. 'Oh, I'm sure you are. I didn't mean, that is—it must be lovely to have two homes.'

He looked as though he were about to say something, but he smiled faintly instead. 'Shall we go up to your room?' he suggested.

It was a charming apartment at the end of the landing where it joined a little passage at right angles. The children's rooms were close by as well as a bathroom, the professor told her as he opened the door. Rather to her surprise he came in too and walked over to the latticed window overlooking the wide sweep of grass behind the house. He spoke casually, looking over his shoulder at her.

'I shall be down for the week-end—we will go over to Chifney if you would like that.'

She beamed her pleasure. 'Oh, lovely—could we really? We can see it easily from the road.'

'My intention was to take you to see your step-brother.'

Her smile faded. 'Then I'd rather not go,' she told him uncertainly. 'It's awfully nice of you to have thought of it, but I don't want to see him.'

'You are afraid of him?' His voice was bland.

She considered the question carefully. 'No—not at all, but I dislike him very much. He was unkind to my mother after my father died.'

'And unkind to you too?' His voice had an edge to it.

'Yes, and William. That's why we've never gone back—you see, he might gloat.'

'Ah yes. All the same, would it not be an excellent opportunity to—er—drop in on him in passing? We might mention William's success in the medical world—a little shop window dressing, as it were. Perhaps we might alter his ideas about you; presumably he thinks of you as a pair of struggling workers, trying to make ends meet.'

'But that's just what we are.' She was incurably honest.

'You know that, and so do I. But we could, without deviating too much from the truth, give him a different picture. Success, my dear girl—a gentle hint that you neither require his help nor wish for it.'

Beth eyed him in some astonishment. 'I should never have guessed...that is, I can't think why you should be so interested.'

There was a gleam of amusement in his eyes. 'Shall we say that I like to see justice done?' he answered mildly, and strolled to the door. 'Lunch in five minutes, and I'll bring the children down with me.'

He nodded pleasantly to her and left her to her thoughts.

They were waiting for her when she returned from taking up Mevrouw Thorbecke's tray, the children unnaturally tidy, the professor lying back in a great easy chair with his eyes shut, but at Beth's appearance he got up and ushered everyone across the hall into the dining room, and the children, finding their tongues, chattered like magpies, but peace reigned again after a few minutes; Mrs Burge was a splendid cook and they all did justice to her roast beef. It wasn't until they were nicely embarked on the apple pie and cream that the conversation, from a polite trickle, became a flood once more. Beth, helping Alberdina and eating her own lunch, felt happier than she had done for a long time. Happy wasn't quite the right word, content was nearer the mark; a pleasant feeling of being somewhere where she was wanted and where she wanted to be. She heaved a sigh of pleasure and caught her host's eye.

'The house first or the animals?' he asked.

She was conscious of four pairs of anxious eyes turned upon her.

'The animals,' she said promptly, and was rewarded by the children's faces.

They went to the pond first, beyond the stables, and fed the ducks there, and then the geese who came waddling towards them, and when the children were tired of that they went down to the wide gate which shut in the donkey and the horses.

'You ride?' asked the professor, holding Alberdina firmly perched on the gate's top rung.

Beth paused, remembering. 'Oh, yes—Beauty, and Sugar when we were children, but that's years ago. What about the children?'

'Not yet; their father wishes them to learn—it might be a good opportunity to get them started if I can find a pony. If you care to ride, please do so. Mrs Burge's son, Jack, looks after things here, he'll saddle either Prince or Kitty for you.'

She glowed, her eyes a deep purple with excitement. 'Oh, how very kind of you! Before breakfast, perhaps? And if you could find a pony, I could start the children off.'

They were strolling round the garden now, with the children darting from one side to the other, delighted with themselves and everything there. As they reached the garden door into the house, the professor stopped.

'This is where I cry off,' he remarked. 'The children will show you the house.'

He didn't say why he wouldn't come with them; ten minutes later, from the landing window, Beth saw him get into his car and drive away. Naturally he would have friends in the neighbourhood; as she was led in and out of the delightful rooms in the old house, she was seeing him very clearly in her mind's eye, being entertained by elegantly dressed lovelies, amusing him with their witty conversation and capturing his attention with their good looks. The hussies, declared Beth silently, quite carried away by her own imagination.

He reappeared that evening just as she had got the children comfortably settled for the night and taken up Mevrouw Thorbecke's tray. She was on her way downstairs, feeling lonely and a little subdued after the children's bracing society, when she heard the car draw up, and a moment later the professor was in the hall, grinning up at her.

'Hullo,' he greeted her, 'am I too late to say good night to those brats?'

She shook her head. 'Not really, though I have just turned out the lights.'

He was already on the stairs. 'Good. I'll be very quick—wait for me in the drawing room, Beth.'

She chose a chair by the splendid empty fireplace and sat composedly, sure in her mind that he wouldn't be staying for dinner, but go away again, leaving her alone.

She found the idea so disagreeable that she stopped thinking about it and pondered instead on his strange habit of calling her by such a variety of names: Beth, Elizabeth, Miss Partridge—Could it be according to his mood? she was wondering, when he joined her.

'Sherry? I'm sure you've earned it. I felt like a traitor leaving you to the mercy of the children for the rest of the day.'

She accepted the sherry. 'I don't suppose you gave it a thought,' she observed coolly.

He had taken a chair opposite her. 'Why do you say that?'

Her voice was sedate. 'I expect you were in pleasant company.'

His eyes had been half shut, now he opened them wide and she was startled afresh at their vivid blue.

'Oh, very pleasant,' he smiled charmingly. 'I have a number of friends living round and about, though I don't see them very often. Perhaps we will have a small party before you go back.'

'A good idea,' she agreed. 'It would do Mevrouw Thorbecke good.'

'And you, Miss Partridge?'

'Me? Oh, you don't have to invite me, Professor. I'm here to look after the children.' She smiled at him warmly.

He put down his glass and got to his feet, took her glass from her hand, too and pulled her upright. 'Will you come if I ask you?' he wanted to know.

'Well, yes, I suppose so,' and because that sounded ungracious: 'Thank you, I should like that—if you want me to come.'

'I want you to come, Beth.' He had bent to kiss her before she realized that that was his intention, tucked his arm under hers and said cheerfully: 'Dinner, I think, don't you? Then I must be off.'

They dined in a leisurely fashion which gave the lie to the professor's intention to leave immediately after the meal, and the conversation, to Beth's secret annoyance, was of nothing but St Elmer's; the newest techniques and surgery in general. He could have been giving a lecture at the hospital instead of sitting at the head of their own elegantly appointed dining table. She felt put out; she might not be much to look at, but no one had ever hinted that she was a dull companion. Perhaps he found talking to her difficult and so kept to safe mutual topics? Her answers became more and more wooden, but he seemed not to notice; he finished a learned and lengthy discourse on the hazards of transplants, looked at his watch and announced that he would have to go. Beth went to the door with him and wished him good-bye and watched him go upstairs to see his sister, before going along to the kitchen to warn Mrs Burge that they had finished their dinner; she took care to stay there until she heard the front door close behind him.

She was crossing the hall on her way to see if the

children were asleep when the professor walked in again. He crossed the hall rapidly to her and Beth stood still, wondering why he had returned.

'That was a ridiculous waste of time at dinner,' he remarked to surprise her. 'What is it about you which prevents me from saying what I wish to say?' He frowned, kissed her thoughtfully and went away again, leaving her standing there, listening to the sound of the car's engine diminishing into the distance.

The week rolled away at a leisurely pace, with the children to fill her days and any time there was over taken up by Mevrouw Thorbecke, who felt better with each successive day. She was good company now that she was almost herself once more and Beth found it no hardship to forego her free time in order to drive her into Shepton Mallet or Castle Cary to shop, or spend a little time exploring the country roads around these two little towns. The elderly estate car in the garage suited her very well, for although she had driven for several years she was very out of practice, but as both of them enjoyed tooling along quietly while they talked about a great many things, that hardly mattered.

Mevrouw Thorbecke was well enough to entertain her friends by now, too. They came after tea and played bridge, so that Beth was free to go out with the children again before their supper; down to the pond to feed the ducks or take carrots to the donkey and sometimes to play ball.

It was Friday evening when the professor came again, arriving silently and putting the car in the garage while she and the children were feeding the ducks. They were on their way upstairs to tidy themselves for supper when he came to his study door, and stood, patient and laughing, while they milled around him, and Beth, watching quietly, was conscious that she was just as glad to see him as the children were, although her, 'Good evening, Professor,' was staid enough.

She saw him later, at dinner. For some reason which she hadn't gone into too deeply, she had elected to wear a woollen dress, by no means new and of an uninteresting brown which did nothing for her at all, and even if she hadn't known this already, his appraising glance and quick dismissal of her person would have told her so; she had a kind of wry pleasure from it, as though she had proved something to herself, as she sat between him and his sister, taking part in the conversation without essaying to draw attention to herself.

'Your day off tomorrow, Elizabeth,' the professor told her. 'You should by rights have two, and from what Martina tells me, you seem to have had precious little time to yourself this week. Can you be ready by ten o'clock tomorrow?'

'Can I be ready at ten…' she repeated stupidly. 'Why?'

'We're going out together. I need your advice about something I want to buy.'

'Oh, birthday presents or something? Yes, of course I can be ready.'

He nodded briefly. 'Good.'

It was only afterwards, when she was getting ready for bed after a pleasant evening in the sitting room, talking idly and listening to the record player, that she remembered, that although he had offered a day off he had at the same time taken it for granted that she would spend some hours of it helping him with his shopping, although upon reflection, she had to admit that she didn't mind in the least.

It was a fine morning again; she put on a jersey dress of a deep mauve which matched her eyes and went down to breakfast, where she was forced to sit under the reproachful gaze of four pairs of eyes. They were not jealous of her going out with their uncle, Dirk was quick to explain, but they would miss her, a remark which touched her very much. It was better when the professor sat himself down with an apology for being late and the remark that if they behaved themselves he had a treat in store for them. All the same, the little group looked glum when it assembled to wish them good-bye as they got into the car. Beth, settling herself beside the professor, said: 'This is smashing, but I feel frightfully guilty about leaving the children—after all, it is Saturday.'

'As you say, it is Saturday—your Saturday too, Beth, and if I heard aright, you have been their constant companion for the whole week.'

'I enjoyed it,' she assured him.

'You like them?'

'Immensely.'

'So do I—I envy Martina and Dirk—they married young.'

'You should marry, Professor.' She added, 'Someone suitable, of course.'

'How unpleasant that sounds! You consider that I have reached an age when a suitable marriage is all that is left for me?'

'Heavens, no. I'm not sure exactly how old you are, but William said thirty-six—that's not in the least old—just right, in fact.'

'But I do not wish to make a suitable marriage, Miss Partridge—a tepid love and a well ordered life with no ups and down; I would wish for fun, a few healthy quarrels and a love to toss me to the skies.' He turned to look at her, smiling, so that she knew that his words weren't meant to be taken seriously.

'Would you consider yourself to be a suitable wife for me, little Partridge?'

She frowned down her small, beaky nose at him; it didn't matter what he chose to call her, it sounded endearing; and that was a piece of nonsense, she told herself sternly. 'Don't be ridiculous,' she made her voice severe. 'Your wife should be very pretty—no, more than that, beautiful, and wear gorgeous clothes and be charming too. She would have to be interested in your work and run your house—houses—perfectly without bothering you about silly little things, and be a super hostess, too.' She had become quite carried away.

'She sounds like a dead bore to me. One day, Beth, I will tell you exactly what kind of wife I intend to marry.'

It was absurd to feel so unhappy. 'Oh, you have someone in mind?' and then, because she couldn't bear to talk about this dream girl of his, she changed the subject abruptly. 'What do you want to buy?'

'You shall know very shortly, dear girl.'

She was looking about her. 'We're going to Shepton Mallett? That's the turning to Lamyott, if we go a little further we shall pass Chifney.'

'Did I not tell you that I should take you there?'

She smiled widely at him. 'How kind of you to remember, we can get a lovely view as we go past.'

But they didn't go past; he slowed the car as they went through the village to turn in through the well-remembered gates and halt in front of the house. She turned to look at him, not smiling now. 'Oh, why…?' she began.

'You will see, Beth. Come along.' He got out of the car and helped her out too, and with a hand under her arm, walked across the gravel to the door and knocked while she stood beside him, not knowing what to say, looking about her at the familiar garden; it was still beautifully kept—her stepbrother would make sure of that; he might not love Chifney, but it was his now and he loved his own image as the squire. The door opened and she turned to face Mrs Trugg, and at the sight of that well-remembered face with its wrinkles and boot button eyes, she cried: 'Oh, Truggy!' and flung herself into the old woman's arms.

'Miss Beth! Dearie me, what a sight for sore eyes.' She turned those same eyes, very sharp now, on to the professor, adding: 'Good day to you, sir. You'll both come in?'

She held the door wide and they both went inside, the professor's hand still cupping her elbow. 'Oh, Truggy,' said Beth in a soft voice, 'how super to see you again. I suppose my stepbrother and his wife are home?'

'Yes, love.' Mrs Trugg beamed at her, puffing a little, for she was a stout little woman. 'And this gentleman?' she prompted.

'Oh, I'm so sorry…' Beth looked at him apologetically, 'it was seeing Truggy… Professor, this is Mrs Trugg who's been housekeeper here for years and years and is my friend. Truggy, this is Professor van Zeust from Holland.'

Mrs Trugg took the hand he held out. 'Fancy that now—a foreign gentleman,' and Beth, reading the kind old face like an open book, added hastily:

'The professor is a consultant surgeon at St Elmer's, Truggy—he lectures in London but he lives in

Holland. I'm looking after his sister's children for a week or two.'

Mrs Trugg accepted this statement with a placid: 'Fancy that now, and very nice too, Miss Beth—a change from all those nasty operations. Now take the professor into the small sitting-room, dearie, and I'll fetch your brother.'

The room hadn't been changed. Beth went over to look out of the window and asked without looking round: 'Why have you brought me here? I didn't want to come—I said...'

He didn't say anything, and she went on looking out at the garden, quite at a loss, and didn't turn round again until the door opened and Philip came in; he hadn't changed either; he was older, of course, but just as sour as she remembered him to be. He greeted her with chilly politeness, as though she were a complete stranger, shook hands with the professor when she introduced them, and after making some meaningless remark about the weather, said: 'Of course I know of you, Professor—you own Caundle Bubb house, do you not? Quite a showplace, I believe.' He sounded patronizing.

'Is it?—I had no idea.' The professor was at his silkiest and Beth saw Philip frown angrily as she went forward to greet her sister-in-law, who shook hands limply and looked her up and down.

'My dear Elizabeth,' she remarked in a high penetrating voice, 'that dress is at least five years old,' a remark which set Beth's cheeks burning, although she choked back the retort bubbling on her tongue and introduced the professor in a wooden voice.

He shook hands with his hostess and then dropped an arm round Beth's shoulders. 'Beth looks delightful in that colour,' he observed gently, at the same time dismissing the other woman's expensive jersey suit with the faintest curl of his lip, so that Beth, quite diverted by this behaviour, wanted to laugh.

'You must be wondering why we are here.' His voice was courteous, although he managed to convey at the same time the idea that he didn't care less whether they wondered or not. 'You have a mare, Beauty, I believe, and a pony, Sugar. I have four nephews and nieces, anxious to ride, and I am looking for quiet mounts for them; I believe that they would be most suitable for that purpose. I should be glad if you would sell them to me.'

Beth drew a sharp breath and felt the pressure of the professor's hand on her shoulder. 'They must be a good age,' he added, 'but of course they'll not be overworked. My own mounts are too lively for children.'

Philip's voice was sharp. 'I presume Elizabeth put you up to this, Professor, though how she got to hear of it I don't know.'

'Hear of what?' asked Beth in a quiet voice which shook a little.

'They're both going to the knacker's tomorrow morning,' he told her brutally.

She felt the blood drain from her face and it took her a few minutes to find her voice, for rage had choked it, but before she could speak the professor said: 'Indeed? You are not an animal-lover, Mr Partridge? How fortunate that I am in time to buy them from you—if you will state your price.'

'I have no intention of selling them.' Philip had gone very red.

'Making a gift of them to the knacker? In which case I can arrange to buy them from him.' The professor's smile was quite ferocious, although he spoke placidly enough. 'We won't trouble you further.'

It was Margaret Partridge who intervened. 'Of course my husband will sell them to you,' she threw Beth a look of dislike. 'I suppose Elizabeth conned you into this—well, we're well rid of them, eating their heads off—I wish you joy of them!'

'Thank you, Mrs Partridge.' He looked at his unwilling host. 'If you would name the sum you have in mind?'

It was Philip who answered this time, stating a ridiculously high sum which made Beth catch her breath. The professor was a kind man, but surely he wouldn't be prepared to go to such lengths to acquire two elderly animals. He was quite prepared; he wrote a cheque without so much as a lift of the eyebrows and handed it over without comment.

'Perhaps I may telephone my house and arrange transport?' he asked, and when he had done that: 'And now if we might take a look?' he suggested.

They all left the house and walked round the back to the stables, with the professor maintaining a flow of small talk, just as though they were all on the best of terms, but his silence was eloquent when he saw how the mare and the pony were housed; neither had been groomed, and they stood dejectedly, their heads down, in a stable which hadn't been cleaned for a long time. Beth, her teeth clenched against the things she wished to say and didn't because something told her that the professor didn't want her to speak just then, stroked their well-remembered, elderly noses and was overjoyed when they remembered her, while the professor grunted in disgust. Presently she ventured in a small voice: 'Could we wait until the horsebox gets here?' and was deeply satisfied by his decided: 'We could and we shall.'

Which made it obligatory for Margaret to offer them coffee. They sat uneasily in the sitting-room again, with the professor in complete charge of the conversation; a gentle monologue for the most part, leaving them in no doubt as to William's success in his chosen profession, touching lightly on Beth's future career and hinting, too, at their pleasant social lives in London, and having made his point he suggested to Beth that she might like to go and have a few words with Mrs Trugg, adding that he would be sure and let her know when the horse-box arrived.

Beth almost laughed at his high-handed behaviour, but it gave her the opportunity of running down to the kitchen to wish her old friend good-bye.

Truggy was waiting for her, making a cake on the scrubbed kitchen table.

'Oh, Miss Beth,' she said eagerly. 'I did hope you'd be able to have a word with me—so lovely it is to see you again, dearie—and that nice gentleman, even if he is foreign.'

Beth perched on the table and began scraping the cake mixture from the bowl with a forefinger and licking it off. 'Truggy, do you know what he's done? He's bought Sugar and Beauty—we're waiting for transport for them—he paid an unheard-of price for them.' Her voice shook. 'Truggy, Philip said he was going to send them to the knackers!'

'That's right, Miss Beth, and so he was. Wicked, I call it, after all these years—but now they'll be safe. No heart, that stepbrother of yours, no heart at all.'

She looked so sad that Beth asked: 'Truggy, when are you going to retire?'

'Well, love, I must wait until I can get my pension—that's another year or more.'

'But, Truggy, why must you wait? Couldn't Philip give you your pension now—and there's the lodge at the back gates—Father promised you that.'

Mrs Trugg snorted. 'That I know, Miss Beth, but what your dear father promised and what your step-brother does are two different things. I'm not to have a pension or get the lodge. It's let, anyway, to some fancy friends of his who pay him a good rent for it.'

'But, Truggy—your pension—he must give you one...'

'There's no must about it, dearie, but don't you worry your head about me. Tell me about Master William and that flat of yours—and how came you here in the first place?'

Beth plunged into an account of William's success and how comfortably they were living in the flat, and if she painted their lives rather more vividly than they were, it was for Truggy's sake. But while she talked she was wondering what she could do to help her old friend; to speak to Philip or Margaret would be of no use at all; she would have to talk to William when she got back to London. She was still worrying about it when the sitting-room bell jangled above the old-fashioned dresser—a signal that she should return to the sitting-room.

'I must go, Truggy,' she spoke reluctantly, 'but William and I will think of something—some way...' She kissed Mrs Trugg and went back upstairs.

The professor got to his feet as she went in and greeted her with an easy: 'Are you ready, dear girl? Jack has just arrived with the horsebox, shall we see it loaded and be off ourselves?'

Beth made her brief farewells and watched as the professor made his; he wasn't being arrogant—not quite, but he wasn't being more than coldly polite either and underneath his bland exterior she sensed contempt, and thought that Philip did too.

Her stepbrother accompanied them to the stables, watching while Jack loaded Sugar and Beauty, and Beth, standing silently by the professor, was terrified that at the last minute something would go wrong and Philip would refuse after all to let the professor have them. She sighed loudly as the land rover with the horsebox in tow, disappeared down the drive on its way to Caundle Bubb, and her companion, making a second, cursory leave of Philip, looked at her and smiled, although he didn't speak to her as they got into the car. It wasn't until they were driving through the village that he spoke.

'Well, that was a near thing, wasn't it?' and then, gently: 'Don't cry, Miss Partridge.'

'The beast!' said Beth on a furious sob. 'The b-beast, he was going to have Sugar and Beauty put down—they've been there ever since I can remember—how could he be so cruel and callous—and that stable, it was awful. I could kill him!'

'Oh, indeed, so could I,' the professor spoke mildly, but all the same she believed him, 'but I fancy that with care and gentle exercise and a little attention from the vet, they will live for a number of years yet.'

Beth sniffed and mopped her eyes. 'I'll never be able to thank you enough. You really do want them, don't you? They will do for the children?'

'Of course. I'm hoping that you will be able to give them their first lesson before you go back to St Elmer's.'

'That would be simply super.' She relapsed into silence and began to think about Mrs Trugg.

'Something is worrying you?' He gave her a long, sidelong glance; the violet eyes were quite something even in her blotchy face. 'Tell me,' he invited.

It seemed the most natural thing in the world to take him at his word. 'It's Truggy,' she started, and out it all came; the lodge that Mrs Trugg wasn't to have after all; and no pension and nowhere to go, and how was she going to live on the OAP and the few pounds she had saved. None of it was very lucid, but he seemed to understand and his questions, though few, cleared up the muddled bits.

'Quite shocking,' he commented, and meant it, 'but there must be a solution, Elizabeth, and I have no doubt that we shall discover it.'

'Yes, I know, but I can't think what—she would hate to come and live in London. I'll have to think of something. Thank you for being so kind about it.'

'There is a little time before your brother is likely to give her notice?'

'Oh yes—I believe so, even he wouldn't dare to give her a week's notice.'

'A great deal can be done in a week or two—will you leave it to me, Beth, and try not to worry about it?'

'But I can't allow you…'

'Please?' and when she nodded with a wonderful sense of relief: 'Good, now let us have lunch. I promise you that when I have thought of something I will tell you at once.'

They lunched at Bowlish House in Shepton Mallett, at a table in one of the elegant windows overlooking the gardens, and although Beth hadn't felt hungry, she ate the beef olives Provençal and apple pie and cream with a healthy appetite, and, assured that it would not go to her head, drank a second glass of claret, while her companion talked cheerfully about the fun the children would have learning to ride, and egging her on in an unobtrusive manner to tell him about Beauty and Sugar and the fun she had had as a child.

On the way back to Caundle Bubb she found herself feeling quite lighthearted; somehow the professor had taken her worries on to his own broad shoulders and she had no doubt at all that he would resolve them for her. She hadn't felt so happy for years.

CHAPTER SIX

THEY all spent a glorious afternoon; there was no question of riding Beauty or Sugar right away, but for the moment at least the children were content to admire them, stroking their noses and offering sugar lumps while Beth, the professor and Jack explained the fine points of grooming a horse and the intricacies of its harness, and when the vet arrived the whole party, by now augmented by the presence of Mevrouw Thorbecke, crowded round and watched while he examined the two animals. He found nothing much wrong; elderly of course and neglected, but with good feeding and regular grooming and gentle exercise they should be good for several years yet. Reassured, everyone trooped in to tea, leaving Jack to settle his charges comfortably, and the rest of the day was spent, by the children at least, in planning a colourful and improbable future for themselves and their new pets.

The success of Sunday was a foregone conclusion; the morning was largely spent hovering round the stables and the adjoining paddock, while Beth and Jack, with the children's enthusiastic assistance, groomed the animals. It was astonishing how quickly they were recovering after barely one day's proper care, and on Monday, Beth promised, she would show the children how to harness Sugar and Beauty, and perhaps by the next day Sugar would be fit enough to ride. Lunch was a decidedly cheerful meal, with the children talking of nothing but horses. 'Which reminds me,' the professor interpolated, 'Prince and I had some exercise before breakfast, but he needs more—so do I—I shall take him out again this afternoon. Would you come with me, Beth? Kitty needs to stretch her legs too. We could go out towards Lovington, along the bridle path. What do you say?'

She looked up from her trifle with a delighted face. 'Oh, I'd love to, but I haven't ridden for years—is Kitty quiet?'

'I keep her specially for my girl-friends; some of them don't ride so very well,' he declared solemnly, a remark which provoked shrieks of laughter from the children and a faint feeling of petulance in Beth.

She had almost forgotten the joys of riding, and Kitty, quiet enough when she needed to be, had a nice turn of speed in the open country. Beth, riding more soberly beside the professor on their way home, declared that she couldn't remember when she had enjoyed herself so much. She was very untidy by now, with her hair hanging around her shoulders and no make-up to speak of; she was wearing slacks and a cotton sweater, neither of them new, and with no riding boots available she had put on a pair of borrowed wellingtons. The professor glanced at her several times, smiling a little, and when they were within sight of Caundle Bubb remarked good-naturedly: 'I'm glad you have enjoyed yourself, Elizabeth, you are a very competent horsewoman.'

She turned to look at him. 'Oh, so that's why you wanted me to come with you—to see if I would be safe with the children, I might have guessed...' She didn't go on. His reason for wanting her company had been so obvious and she hadn't even thought of it; indeed, she had actually imagined that he had wished for her society. It was a lowering discovery.

'Well, that was partly my reason, but only partly, little Partridge. It is a pity that I have already promised to ride with neighbours of ours tomorrow, for I should have enjoyed helping you with the children, but I shall be free in the afternoon and I wondered if we might all go to Cheddar Gorge; the children haven't been there and they will be going home in another week and I promised them a treat. Martina can come with us and if she is tired, she can stay in the car while we take the children into the caves.'

Beth knew the caves well. 'They'll love that,' she assured him warmly. 'I think Gough's cave is the best, don't you, but do you suppose they'll want to see them all?'

'Very probably. It will probably be an exhausting afternoon, but I don't need to leave until after dinner, so we shan't have to hurry.'

She agreed soberly, thinking that in a week's time she would be going back to St Elmer's herself, a reflection which prompted her to ask:

'When do you go back to Holland?'

'Oh, very shortly.'

'For—for good?'

'Lord, no. I come over to England several times in a year, you know, though I don't believe that I am coming to London for quite some time—not, that is, to lecture. Edinburgh, if my memory serves me right, Bristol and Birmingham. I shall spend a few days here, naturally and it is easy enough to come over for a week-end in the London house.' He smiled at her. 'You see, I am partly English, am I not? and I would wish to remain so.'

They were ambling up the drive to the house now and there was no need for her to answer him because the children, on the watch, had seen them and came pouring out to meet them.

The next morning went too quickly; Sugar and Beauty, delighted to be among friends again, allowed themselves to be saddled and bridled and made much of, and then Beth mounted Dirk on Sugar, and herself on Beauty, ambled round the paddock, with the boy, impatient of the leading rein, urging her to go faster.

'No,' said Beth decisively, 'they've got to get quite fit first; you're doing splendidly, Dirk, but think of Sugar; he needs a few more days of rest. Ambling along like this won't hurt either of them and by the time they're quite fit, you'll be good enough to get up on Beauty.'

Dirk was good after that, puffing out his skinny chest, telling his brothers and sisters what Beth had said and so pleased with himself that he waited patiently while she took each of the other children in turn, and then allowed them all to help her groom the beasts. It was difficult to get them away from the stables; if it hadn't been for the prospect of the Cheddar Gorge, she fancied they would have been content to have stayed there all day.

They were playing hide-and-seek in the garden when the professor, riding Prince, came home, and Beth, waiting to be found, concealed behind a box hedge, had the leisure to study him as he came up the drive. He looked good in riding kit and he sat a horse as though he had been born to it—probably he had, she conceded. What was more, he was handsome enough, despite his craggy face, to make any girl look twice at him. She wondered why he hadn't married, and became so engrossed in this interesting fact that she hardly heard Hubert's voice asking his uncle if he had seen her, but she did hear the professor's reply. 'Oh, yes, I've seen her all right, though I imagine she thinks she is nicely hidden—I had a splendid view of her out of the corner of one eye.'

He leaned down as he spoke to take up Hubert and sit him before him on Prince and then wheel the horse so that Hubert could see her too, and set him down again to chase Beth delightedly into the house while he rode on towards the stables.

They set out for the Cheddar Gorge after a hilarious lunch, with the children too excited to eat and even Mevrouw Thorbecke in a gayer mood than Beth had seen her in. The Gorge looked beautiful and a little awe-inspiring in the April afternoon sun, and it was still too early in the year for there to be many visitors. The professor slid the Citroën slowly downhill between the grey rocky cliffs and half-way down pulled in on to the wide grassy verge under overhanging rock. 'Is this a good place to stop?' he wanted to know. 'Martina, are you quite sure you'll be happy in the car for an hour?'

Mevrouw Thorbecke was content enough to be left to read and doze in the warmth of the sun and the party, in lively spirits, started off for the caves.

Beth had almost forgotten how extraordinary they were; she viewed their fairylike interiors, peering at the delicate petrified drops falling perpetually from a roof they could hardly see, and the graceful mounds growing from the ground, and fell into a friendly argument with the professor as to which were stalactites and which stalagmites; the children, who didn't know much about it anyway, joined in and it was a gay party, still talking busily, which emerged into the sunshine again, which somehow made Beth's disappointment all the keener when the professor declared his intention of going back to the car. 'I'm going to take Martina along for a cup of tea,' he told her. 'You can have an hour,' he cautioned her. 'Surely in that time these brats will have tired themselves out.'

He gave her a casual, friendly nod, and strolled away.

For a little while all went well; the children were passably good, and Beth, scrambling with them along the side of the gorge, was content to let them roam where they wished within limits, but when Dirk declared his intention of climbing the almost sheer face of the cliff above them, she declared in no uncertain terms that he was to do no such thing. But an imp of mischief had got into the boy; he danced away, shouting that he would do just what he liked; that the cliff was easier than anything else in the world to climb, and that she had no right to forbid him to enjoy himself.

'OK,' said Beth, realizing that guile was necessary, 'so you're hard done by. A pony to ride, a lovely holiday and no school for weeks, a visit to the caves—you're definitely underprivileged.'

'What's underprivileged?' asked Marineka.

Beth explained hastily and then added coaxingly: 'Come on, Dirk, you can't leave us to go back alone, you know—you're the eldest and you're in charge.'

He wavered, then 'No, I'm not, you are—you're grown up and we're only children.'

He pulled a hideous grimace at her and started off, his hands in his pockets. From the back he looked very like a miniature of his uncle. Beth stifled the thought and called: 'Come back, Dirk!' in a no-nonsense voice and just for a moment she thought that he would obey her, but: 'I'm old enough to do what I like!' he shouted after a long moment, and made for a narrow grass-covered cleft, running up between the cliffs. It wasn't too dangerous at first because there were plenty of foot-holds and it was narrow enough for anyone climbing it to get hand-holds on the rock on either side, but a hundred feet further it shot steeply on to a small plateau and after that the going looked hazardous.

Beth wasn't a climber herself and she had no idea if Dirk was good at it, but to rush after him would be foolish; he would merely climb higher in order to get away from her; remembered episodes with William when they were children made her certain of that. What had begun as a prank had become grim earnest. She turned her back on him and saw that the other children were standing and staring upwards at their brother; any minute now, she thought a little desperately, Hubert will decide to have a go as well. She said loudly and in a confident voice: 'He'll come down again in a minute or two, my dears—he's just going as far as that little grassy platform.' She spoke reassuringly while she thought hard. The hour the professor had suggested was almost up; if they didn't go back to the car within a reasonable time she felt sure that he would come in search of them. If Dirk wasn't going to come down the children would have to be left at the base of the cleft while she went after him and with any luck at all, the professor would be in time to get Dirk— and herself down before they had gone very far. They might even get back before he turned up.

She sent an urgent prayer skywards and looked over her shoulder. Dirk had reached the plateau and when he saw her looking, waved defiantly and began the more hazardous climb towards the very top of the cliff. There was no path as far as she could see, and no grass; the very thought of having to go after him made her feel sick, but there was nothing else to do. Even if they all hurried back to the car and fetched the professor, who might not be there, Dirk could have missed his footing and fallen. She turned to Marineka, making her voice casual.

'I think I'll go and give Dirk a hand, dear—will you stay here and look after Hubert and Alberdina until we get back or your uncle comes? I shall be able to see you and you can watch us. Only promise to stay exactly here—we'll be back in the wink of an eye.'

If I get back at all, she told herself silently as she started up the cleft. Dirk was far above her now and she wondered if she was a fool to follow him—perhaps he was a born climber and quite fearless, in which case she would be doing more harm than good and terrifying herself to no purpose. She climbed steadily and when she reached the plateau she made herself look down on the children and wave; the ground looked a long way away and it seemed to her that it would probably be Dirk who brought her down and not the other way round.

She drew a calming breath and started up the cliff face. Dirk was nowhere to be seen, but there was a jutting point of rock ahead of her, he would be beyond that and hidden from her. She clawed her way along, forcing herself to look ahead and not down, and trying not to think of having to climb down again. There was a narrow ledge running round the spur, the cliff towering on one side of it, a steep slope, peppered with outcrops of rock, falling to the ground on the other. She peeped at it fearfully, giddy with fright, her heart thumping so loudly that it almost deafened her, but not quite; she still heard Dirk's voice, quite close, coming from the other side of the spur and there was no defiance in it now. 'Beth—oh, Beth, I'm so glad you've come—I'm stuck and I feel sick.' He added a great deal more, but it was in Dutch and she couldn't understand a word of it.

That makes two of us, she thought wryly, and said aloud in a strong cheerful voice: 'Oh, I'm sure you're not stuck—can you come round to this side and we'll go down together.' She lied brightly: 'It's quite easy.'

'I can't.'

'Then hold on, and I'll come round.'

She had no idea afterwards how she did it, she was so terrified now that she was stiff with fear; if she had been on her own she would never have made the attempt; as it was, she found herself standing beside Dirk on an even narrower ledge which just disappeared into the rock face, so that there was nowhere to go even if she had been brave enough to attempt to do so. Dirk was standing with his face to the cliff, holding on to its rough surface with desperate hands, and she got as near to him as she dared and slid an arm across his shoulders so that he was in its shelter; it was of no earthly use, but it might make him feel more secure.

'That's better,' she spoke in a voice which she willed to be steady. 'We'll wait for a bit, shall we? When we've got our breath we'll have a shot at getting back.'

'I can't.'

'Well, perhaps not, just at this moment, but later…anyway, someone will be bound to see us and come and give us a hand.' She could hear the occasional car going up or down the gorge below, and she imagined that she could hear the children calling too, but that would be fancy. She hoped that they hadn't taken fright and gone tearing off in search of their uncle and mother and got lost—knocked down by a car, fallen over…a stream of horrifying possibilities followed each other swiftly across her frightened mind, each one a little worse than the last, and when she told herself not to be a fool, that didn't help at all. But there was nothing to be gained by working herself into a panic; they had been there for hours—well, minutes, at least, the professor would surely have come in search of them by now.

'Oh, please do let him hurry…' She had spoken out loud, and thinking about it later, it hadn't seemed in the least strange when he answered her. His voice was cool and unhurried and came from the other side of the spur. 'My dear Miss Partridge, I'm being as quick as I can, but you really must make allowances for my age.' Half of his vast person appeared round the spur and she could have cried with relief.

'Boy,' commanded the professor, 'take your hand from the rock and catch hold of mine. Beth, make yourself small so that he can get between you and the cliff face—can you do that?'

It was extraordinary, but she felt capable of doing anything at that moment and although she was still frightened she felt safe. She did exactly as she had been told and Dirk inched himself past her and she heard the professor telling him what to do, only since he spoke in Dutch, it made no sense to her, but whatever it was, it must have been successful for very shortly afterwards he said: 'Now your turn, my dear girl; take a good hold of my hand and edge towards me without turning round; it's quite easy going round the spur. Take your time; I've got Dirk hanging on to my other hand.'

Her mind boggled at the picture this remark conjured up, but she obeyed him with a desperate calmness and found herself on the other side of the spur, squashed against him. 'Ah, splendid,' boomed the professor, still very cheerful. 'Now we can go back to the others.'

She wasn't sure how she managed that either, and she wondered once or twice how the professor felt about it, for he had each of them by the hand and nothing to hold on to. The little plateau looked like heaven when they reached it, but he didn't allow them to pause, going on down the gully, with Dirk, now that they were reasonably near the ground, gaining confidence at every step. As for herself, she wanted to be sick.

On the ground at last, they were surrounded by the children, who obviously regarded the whole episode as a splendid joke and looked admiringly at Dirk, who now that he was safe was inclined to boast about his climb. But his uncle cut him short and marshalled them into a tidy little party and started back towards the car, warning them, in a voice which brooked no disobedience, that they were to say nothing until he told them that they might, and in a much gentler voice he asked

Beth if she felt all right, and when she nodded, not trusting herself to speak, he smiled very kindly at her. 'You're quite a girl,' he told her, and tucked a hand under her elbow and kept it there, a very welcome support, until they reached the car.

The children didn't breathe a word during the drive back, nor during their tea; indeed, they were quite subdued because their mother had developed a headache and had gone to her room to lie down, but the professor was much as usual, only Beth noticed that he had very little to say to Dirk.

She wasn't surprised when she was asked to go to the professor's study after the meal; he would want to know exactly what had happened—besides, she wanted to thank him for rescuing them and this would be a splendid opportunity to do so without an audience. But once in the study, facing him across the desk, things were rather different; the face he turned to hers was kind and impersonal, as was his voice.

'Now, if I might have this afternoon's escapade explained to me?' he invited. He sounded courteous; prepared to be fair, and a stranger.

Beth studied him, trying to decide what to say. Undoubtedly, Dirk would be punished if she gave him the full story; on the other hand the professor wasn't a man to be fobbed off with a botched-up tale. 'There's nothing much to tell,' she said at length. 'It was rather as Dirk told you...'

She wished she hadn't said that because he said at once, 'Ah, yes—that jumbled account I was given on the way to the car. It was the boy's fault, wasn't it? Was he rude? Disobedient? He endangered your life as well as his own.' His expression softened. 'You're not much of a climber, are you, little Partridge?'

Why did little Partridge sound like an endearment? She answered him quietly: 'No, I'm hopeless at anything like that. I thought Dirk was pretty good. Boys...'

'No red herrings, Elizabeth,' his voice was blandly amused. 'You aren't going to tell me anything, are you? Was it your fault?'

She considered this question carefully. 'No, I don't think so, if you mean was I being unreasonable or bad-tempered or something, but I'd rather not say any more, and if you're going to punish Dirk, please don't—he had an awful fright.'

He ignored this. 'And you, Beth, did you have an awful fright?'

'Ghastly—you see, I'm pure coward.' She smiled at him. 'I thought you'd never come.'

He got up and came round the desk and bent to lift her chin with a compelling forefinger. 'But you knew that I would. And you're not a coward; never that— loyal and bossy and soft-hearted and as obstinate as a mule when the occasion arises, and honest...' He stood up, towering above her. 'Now I'm going to talk to young Dirk and then I shall go to his mother and give her an expurgated version of this afternoon's little adventure and I hope I may rely on you to back me up—and don't worry, I'll see that the children don't terrify her with their own highly coloured versions.'

She got up. 'How can you possibly stop them?'

'I shall bribe them.'

'But that's wrong!' She was quite shocked.

'I know—I often do things which are wrong; don't you, dear girl? Indeed, lately I have found myself doing and thinking a number of strange things—I expect it's something to do with my stars.'

'Stars?'

He nodded. 'You're a West Country woman—do you not remember: "A star looks down at me and says: Here am I and you. Stand, each in our degree. What do you mean to do?"'

'Thomas Hardy,' she said mechanically. 'I didn't think you were like this.' Her pansy eyes searched his face and she made no attempt to explain what she meant, but he understood, for he said gently: 'But you do not know me, Beth.'

'No. Do you know what you mean to do?'

'Oh, yes, but it needed a star to point the way, as it were—a man gets a little set in his ways, you know.'

She was going to have to go over this conversation very carefully later on; it could mean something or nothing at all, but it seemed suddenly very important that she should know which it was. She would have liked to have asked him a great deal more, but she guessed that he wanted to talk to Dirk, and if he was leaving after dinner, there wasn't much time. 'I haven't thanked you yet,' she said, 'and I should like to do that. I—we were so glad to see you—you'll never know…'

'Shan't I? I was rather hoping you would tell me about that.' But he made no attempt to delay her as she reached the door.

She was busy after that, getting Alberdina ready for bed and then seeing to the children's supper. There was no sign of Dirk and she made no attempt to find him; the less said about his interview with his uncle the better. He turned up when the meal was half finished, and ate silently amidst his sisters' and brother's chatter, and when the dressing-gowned Alberdina and Hubert had gone to say good night to their mother and Marineka was getting ready for bed, Beth ventured to ask: 'Your uncle wasn't cross, Dirk?'

She was quite shocked at the look he gave her; childish rage she could understand, but this was something more; dislike, contempt… 'Why should you want to know? So that you can feel pleased with yourself?'

She gaped at him. 'Dirk, what a funny thing to say! Why should I be pleased? And after our dreadful fright this afternoon…'

She had said the wrong thing, for he told her in a furious voice that he hadn't been in the least frightened. He hunched his shoulders in a manner which reminded her forcibly of William in his younger days when he had been caught out in some naughtiness, and asked if he might leave the table. 'I shall go to bed,' he informed her, and wished her a cold good night.

Beth piled the plates on to a tray, ready for Mrs Burge to carry away. 'Good night, Dirk,' she said cheerfully. 'We'll go riding tomorrow.'

He didn't answer, and his mouth was set in such a stubborn line that she hardly expected one. She saw all the children into their beds presently and bade them good night, then went along to her room to change her dress. The green one, she decided, and brushed her hair until it gleamed like copper and did her face with special care. A great waste of time, actually, because when she went into the sitting-room the professor was on the point of going. Mevrouw Thorbecke was lying on one of the sofas and they were speaking Dutch, although they switched at once to English as he wished his sister good-bye, gave her a brotherly peck on her cheek, then took a businesslike leave of Beth. She was conscious of disappointment as she heard the door close behind him, and this turned to peevishness when her companion, over their dinner, told her that he had decided to leave a few hours earlier so that he could call on friends on his way. Friends, thought Beth, crossly, he had been riding with a friend, hadn't he— another girl, most likely, someone he couldn't bear to tear himself away from. She frowned so fiercely at her soup that Mevrouw Thorbecke asked her if she didn't like it. After that she didn't think about him any more but laid herself out to be a pleasant companion; she was beginning to think too much about the man.

The week went by, too fast. No one had said anything to her, but the agreed time had been two weeks and Saturday would be the last day; on Friday evening Beth packed her case and when she had put the children to bed, went down to join their mother for dinner. Something would surely be said during the meal, and if it wasn't she would give a little prompting; Mevrouw Thorbecke was charming and she liked her, but she had, Beth guessed, been looked after and cherished all her life; probably the professor had made all her decisions for her before she got married, and her husband doubtless did the same. It was likely that she took it for granted that the matter of Beth's departure would be taken care of by someone, and that the necessary arrangements would be made without bothering her.

They were beginning on Mrs Burge's excellent watercress soup when they heard the gentle swish of the Citroën's tyres, and a minute or so later the professor's step in the hall.

Mevrouw Thorbecke looked pleased. 'That is nice,' she observed. 'Alexander did not think that he would get here until tomorrow, now he will be able to see how well the children have progressed with their riding.'

She lifted her face for his kiss as he joined them and

Beth answered his greeting with a relieved smile; now perhaps she would hear something definite about going back. If she stayed just long enough to put the children through their paces on Sugar and Beauty, she would still be able to catch the early afternoon train to Yeovil; she could be at St Elmer's by the evening and back at the flat in time to get the supper. The prospect didn't appeal; she didn't want to go back. She was contemplating the idea sourly in her mind's eye when the professor's voice disturbed her unhappy train of thought.

'Martina has spoken to you about going back?' he wanted to know.

'Well, no—not yet. I thought, that is, I expected that we might talk about it this evening. I have packed...' She faltered to a halt because of the surprise on his face. 'We did say two weeks,' she pointed out.

He sat back to allow Mrs Burge to remove his soup plate. 'So we did. Tell me, Beth, are you so anxious to return to your hospital duties?'

'No, I'm not,' she was quite certain about it. 'It's been absolutely super here, but I have to go back and that's that.' Sadness at leaving compounded of a mixture of the old house, the children, their mother, Sugar and Beauty, and last but by no means least, the professor, almost choked her.

'You have told the children that you are going?' He was carving the saddle of lamb with negligent skill and wasn't looking at her.

'No, as a matter of fact, I haven't. I thought I'd tell them after they had had their riding lesson in the morning. If I caught the train to Yeovil directly after lunch they wouldn't have time to—to think about it.'

'Never mind the train. Martina wants you to go to Holland with her and the children for a week or two more.' He gave his sister a tolerant smile. 'But it seems she hadn't got around to saying anything about it to you. She has a way of leaving everything to arrange itself at the last minute, knowing that someone or other will make sure that it does.'

Mevrouw Thorbecke laughed apologetically. 'Alexander is right, Beth. That is exactly what I do, and I am ashamed that I haven't asked you sooner, but most truly I would wish you to come with us—just for a little while. I do not know how I shall manage without you—in another week or so I shall be quite able to cope with the children, even without a nanny— besides, my husband will be home very shortly.' A charming smile lit her face. 'Please, Beth!'

Beth made no attempt to hide her delight; indeed, it would not have entered her head to do so, although she felt bound to point out one or two obstacles to the plan. 'But they're expecting me back,' she pointed out, 'and there's William…'

The professor laid down his knife and fork. 'There will be no objection to you being loaned to Martina for another few weeks,' he stated positively, 'and as for

William, this arrangement he now has—could it not be continued for a little longer? Look, I'll tell you what I'll do; run you back to St Elmer's when I go on Sunday; you can spend a couple of days at your flat and I'll pick you up on our way over to Holland.'

It was all so easy it would have been churlish to refuse, although Beth suspected that the ease had been well planned beforehand. It must have given him a good deal of trouble, although less trouble perhaps than finding someone else to help Mevrouw Thorbecke until she was on her feet once more. 'Well,' she said at last, 'if nobody minds me going and you really want me, I'd like to come very much—until you can find someone else.'

The professor resumed his dinner with the air of a man who had pulled off a tricky deal to his own advantage, and Mevrouw Thorbecke, beaming with satisfaction, plunged at once into details of their impending journey.

Several times during the evening Beth detected a look of almost smug satisfaction upon the professor's handsome face, which somehow disturbed her; had she been too easy to persuade? she wondered. Very likely he was in the habit of using his wealth and influence—and his undoubted charm—in getting what he wished for; she had been far too quick to jump at his offer. But when they parted at bedtime, and he thanked her in his kind way, she forgot her disquiet.

He was a dear, she reflected as she went upstairs, and always so calm and good-natured. She wondered what he would be like if ever he lost his temper, for she felt sure that beneath that calm he was capable of a fine rage. She dismissed the thought, for she was unlikely to witness such an occasion, and with rather more difficulty dismissed her thoughts of the professor too.

CHAPTER SEVEN

BETH was awakened the next morning by a gentle tapping on her door. It was far too soon to get up, and supposing it to be one of the children she called: 'Come in,' and started from her bed, only to jump back in again at the professor's: 'I'll do no such thing—think of my reputation. I'm taking Prince out, would you like to keep me company on Kitty?'

She was already out of bed again. 'Give me ten minutes,' she begged him, and fell to tearing into her clothes.

He was standing by the open door when she got downstairs, looking out into the early morning. He had his back to her so that she had the time to notice his well cut jodhpurs, highly polished riding boots and polo-necked sweater; they made her cast a surreptitious glance at her own workaday person and reminded her that she had bothered with neither make-up nor a proper hair-do; indeed, her hair, though brushed, hung in a plait down her back, fastened haphazardly with an elastic band. But the professor didn't appear to notice these shortcomings, only greeted her placidly, observed that they should have a splendid ride on such a fine morning, and led the way to the stables.

As indeed they did; there was very little traffic on the roads, only the postman and the milkman and the awkward, slow-moving farm vehicles. They took to the bridle path presently, which would bring them round to the other side of the village, not hurrying, but ambling along side by side when there was room, talking idly about nothing in particular. Presently the professor asked: 'There was no opportunity to ask you yesterday evening—how are Sugar and Beauty?'

'In splendid shape—you have no idea how different they look already, and the children are splendid with them—Dirk has been on Beauty and goes very well. Marineka was a little timid at first, but she's over that now. Hubert and Alberdina only ride Sugar, of course; I think he enjoys it as much as they do.'

'That's splendid. I found your stepbrother a very unpleasant man, if you will forgive me for saying so.'

'He is. It was lovely to watch you flatten him.'

'My dear girl, was it so obvious?' He turned to grin at her. 'I thought I was being very civil.'

'Oh, you were, but you have a very arrogant manner sometimes.'

'Not with you, I hope?'

She considered his question. 'No—you have always been very kind.'

'Lord, what a quenching remark! Besides, I can be very unpleasant too—I have a vile temper.'

She looked at him with interest. 'I was wondering that...but you control it, don't you? I think you're very nice,' she told him simply.

He had gone ahead of her, for the path was narrow and she had only a brief glimpse of his face as he glanced over his shoulder. 'Thank you, little Partridge,' was all he said.

She put the children through their paces after breakfast with their mother and uncle as an audience, who, when necessary, gave a helping hand. And they did very well, although Dirk was unusually quiet, and when Beth spoke to him, although he answered her politely enough, she was aware of enmity behind the politeness. She was at a loss to know why; she was almost sure that the professor hadn't punished him for his escapade at the Cheddar Gorge and she had never mentioned it. But children could be moody, she consoled herself, probably everything would be all right again in a very short time.

Only it wasn't; Saturday passed and Sunday came with all of them going to church and then, after lunch, having one more ride, and still Dirk maintained his strange behaviour towards her, and when she wished them all good-bye at bedtime with the promise that

they would all meet again in London in two days'
time, he accepted the news with such a lack of enthusiasm that she felt quite dashed. It was fortunate that
the other three were so pleased at the idea of her
coming with them to Holland that she couldn't help but
cheer up, telling herself that everything would be fine
again once Dirk had come out of the sulks.

The professor drove her back to London after
dinner, wasting no time on the journey because, as he
pointed out, he had a heavy list in the morning and in
any case, it was necessary to get her to the flat at a reasonable hour. 'There's no need for you to go to St
Elmer's,' he told her. 'I've arranged everything, I
believe. I finish tomorrow afternoon and shall return
to Caundle Bubb during the evening. We will pick you
up on Tuesday afternoon—half past one at your flat.
You will be ready?'

How businesslike he was! 'Oh, yes, thank you,' she
assured him. 'Which way shall we go?'

'Hovercraft from Dover to Calais and drive up into
Holland from there. Three hours' journey roughly—
we should be in Willemstad in good time to get the
children to their beds.' He glanced at her briefly. 'It's
good of you to come, Elizabeth. I've heard from my
brother-in-law; he hopes to return earlier than he had
expected and I shall be able to relinquish Martina and
the brats to his care once more. She's a good mother
but not very practical—I daresay you've noticed.'

'Yes, but being a good mother is much more important than being practical; besides, she doesn't have to be, does she? It doesn't really matter…'

He finished for her: 'Because there's always someone to see to things for her. You're quite right, of course.'

They talked nothings after that, until he drew up outside the flat, and when Beth would have thanked him and got out, he told her to stay where she was, and got out himself and saw to her luggage and only then opened her door. They went up the stairs together, and after the spacious beauty of Caundle Bubb, it seemed like prison. As he put the key in the lock, she wondered what sort of mess the flat would be in with only William and Dobson to look after it.

It was clean enough, she saw that at a glance, but it looked bleak and unlived-in. There were, naturally, no flowers, and the crockery, though washed, had been piled on the table ready for the next meal. She turned away from this depressing picture and asked diffidently: 'Would you like a cup of coffee?'

He went past her into the kitchen and looked in the fridge, then coolly opened the cupboard and looked in that too. His face bore a look of surprised horror, but all he said was: 'Dear girl, I had no idea; I am so used to Mrs Silver or Mrs Burge or Ria waiting with a meal to serve the moment I get home; evidently William eats out or at the hospital. I told him that you would be back this evening, but he must have forgotten.' He swung her gently round and caught her by the arm. 'Come on, we're going to my house to have a meal.'

There was nothing she would like better; she was hungry and depressed, the idea of sitting alone in this neglected little room, drinking tea with no milk in it, almost moved her to tears. All the same, she said: 'Thank you, but there is no need—you must have a great deal to do—besides, we had dinner before we left.'

He opened his eyes wide. 'But that was hours ago.' He smiled at her and she found herself smiling back and he said: 'That's better—it's only half past ten, you know. Mrs Silver will feed us.'

It was pleasant to be overruled; Beth allowed herself to be led down the dreary staircase again and out to the car. Only when they were seated side by side once more did she venture: 'But your list—does it start at eight?'

'Yes, dear girl, and if you're worrying about a good night's sleep so that I have a nice steady hand in the morning, don't; six hours is enough for me.' He gave her a long look, and said deliberately: 'Don't fill your pretty head with nonsense of that sort.'

He had said 'Don't worry your pretty head,' she had heard him distinctly, and while common sense told her that it was a mere figure of speech, she wished that it had been more than that even while she urged herself not to be so stupid. The professor was a dear; the nicest man she had ever met, but there was no use in getting sentimental about him. She ignored his remark and made a prosaic observation about the Sunday evening traffic.

It was just as he had said; as he put the key in his door Mrs Silver came bustling into the hall with a cheerful: 'There you are, Professor,' and when she saw Beth, 'and you've brought Miss Partridge with you, and a good thing too, for I've got the most delicious pâté of cod's roe waiting for you—I'll bring it to the sitting-room and you can have it on the small table there—the pair of you will be lost in the dining-room.' She beat a retreat and they caught the words 'hot buttered toast,' and 'good strong coffee' as she went back to her kitchen.

The professor caught Beth's eye and grinned disarmingly. 'You see what I mean? I don't deserve it, but I have the most wonderful people to look after me.'

It was on the tip of her tongue to observe that probably he paid the wonderful people very high wages, too, for it was obvious to her after several weeks in his household that he was a wealthy man, although she was forced to admit that even without a penny to his name he would have been offered the same service.

They went into the sitting-room together, where a small round table had been drawn up to a cheerful log fire and the professor urged her gently into a chair beside it before going to a side table, elegantly burdened with decanters and glasses. 'Sherry?' he offered, and when she said yes, brought it to her and sat down close by, to engage her in undemanding conversation until Mrs Silver, standing back with a nod of satisfaction from the table, told them that their meal was ready.

It was a delicious supper, but even if it had been beans on toast and Nescafé, she would have enjoyed it. The professor, when he chose, could be an amusing companion and he had the gift of listening as well as talking; when she looked at the bracket clock above the Adam fireplace, she couldn't believe that it was getting on for midnight.

'The time,' she exclaimed, 'look at the time!'

Her companion remained calm. 'Home in ten minutes, you'll be in bed soon after.'

'Yes, but you—I'm keeping you up, surely I can take a bus?'

'Don't you care for my driving?'

She chuckled. 'Don't be absurd, Professor—you're a very good driver and you know it. I never feel nervous with you.'

'I had noticed. There are girls, you know, who squeal and clutch one's arm at every corner—so trying.'

'I don't suppose you take them out a second time?' Her voice was demure. 'Thank you for my supper. Has Mrs Silver gone to bed?'

'I imagine so—if I had known that you wished for a chaperone, I would have asked her to stay up, Miss Partridge.' He was laughing at her.

'Don't be so silly—I only wanted to thank her for her lovely pâté.'

He was standing close to her, but she didn't look at him.

They didn't say much to each other on the way back to the flat, at the door he got out too and despite Beth's protest, went upstairs with her and saw her into her own flat, but he didn't go in with her this time, only advised her to go to bed at once and wished her a good night. She stood leaning against the door after he had gone, listening to his unhurried steps on the stairs, feeling suddenly tired and dispirited, before taking his advice, and without bothering to unpack, went to bed.

There was a letter in the morning, typed, brief and businesslike. It accompanied a cheque for her two weeks at Caundle Bubb. She read it through several times, seeing not the cold typed words but the kind and considerate man behind them. He would be a perfect husband; she sat at the kitchen table while the kettle boiled and allowed herself the indulgence of day-dreaming—a succession of slightly muddled thoughts, all vague, and brought to an abrupt end by the kettle's whistle. She drank her tea and sat down once more to do sums; any number of them on the back of a paper bag, lying handy. The cheque would pay for William's shoes and a suit besides, for she had spent very little of the first one, and as for herself, she would go shopping the very next morning. She tore round the flat, tidying it up, mopping and dusting and changing beds on a whirlwind of activity. By eleven o'clock the place looked like home again and she was in the kitchen, making bread. She had milk and eggs by now and there were several tins in the cupboard. She was trying to decide what to make from them when William came in, followed by the sheepish Dobson.

Her brother's, 'Hi, Beth,' was hearteningly delighted, and his companion's, 'Hullo, Beth,' while only an echo of William's exuberance, was genuinely pleased. Probably with good cause, she thought, remembering William's efforts at cooking. She greeted them in sisterly tones, offering coffee and asked if they were staying to lunch.

William looked surprised. 'Well, of course— Professor van Zeust told me you'd be back for a couple of days.' He clapped a hand to his head. 'Oh, lord, I meant to have brought some food!'

'I found some tins.' Beth looked at Dobson. 'You'll stay too?'

'I say, may I? You're sure you don't mind? I could easily…'

She smiled at him very kindly. 'There's plenty. You're on again this afternoon, I suppose?'

'Um—and then on call until tomorrow morning and back on duty until teatime, so you won't see us before you go.' William sniffed. 'Can I smell bread?'

'You can—you forgot to buy any.'

They went into the sitting room and had their coffee and she was brought up to date with all the latest hospital news. Only when they had come to an end of this did William ask: 'And how were things with you, Beth?'

'Professor van Zeust didn't tell you?' she asked, and was given a shocked look. 'Good lord, Beth, he's a professor—one of the big boys—he doesn't discuss his private life with the likes of me.'

'Oh, well—I didn't know. Actually, it's been great fun—he took me over to Chifney…' She proceeded to tell them about the visit to Philip and Margaret. 'And you should have seen their faces!' she chortled. 'Professor van Zeust just swept everything along the way he wanted it to go. You ought to see Sugar and Beauty now, they look marvellous.'

'Now aren't you glad I talked you into it, old girl?' her brother wanted to know. 'Any lolly yet, by the way?'

She rose to go into the kitchen. 'Yes, I cashed the cheque this morning. I'll leave some in your room before I go,' and was rewarded for this sisterly thoughtfulness by a flattering: 'Good old Sis—there's a girl I want to take out…'

Beth had heard that one before, many times. 'Do I know her?'

'Harriet King. There's that film on, I've forgotten its name, but I thought we might go.'

'You won't be here, Beth,' struck in the almost silent Dobson. 'I should have liked to have taken you.'

She smiled kindly at him. 'Oh, Dobs, that would have been fun, but I'm leaving again tomorrow afternoon. Now let's eat or you two will be late back.'

It was lucky it was a fine day; Beth did an enormous wash and hung it on the tiny balcony outside the kitchen, then turned her attention to the important matter of what clothes to take with her. It was long past teatime by the time she had decided on the suit, yet again; the violet dress for the good reason that the professor had said that he liked it, and a jersey skirt with a couple of thin sweaters, all of which she intended to supplement in the morning. She ate tea-cum-supper, did the ironing, washed her hair and went to bed, very content.

She was up and out early in the morning, combing the half empty shops for exactly what she wanted; she hadn't had so much money to spend for a long time and it had to be laid out carefully. She was home before midday with everything she had hoped to buy; rather expensive shoes, because she had small, pretty feet and was proud of them, a jersey dress in a quaker grey which made her eyes more purple than they were, slacks from Marks and Spencer and a couple of blouses to go with them—she was perfectly satisfied, and she had spent all the money she had allowed herself.

She packed carefully, put the five pounds she had promised William in his tie drawer, wrote a cheque for the rent and went to have a bath and get ready for her journey, feeling pleased with her small world—there was money in the bank; more than enough for William's needs and a little over for a rainy day, and there were still two weeks to come. Life, she told herself, was good; such a lot of pleasant things had been happening, and all of them since she had met the professor, for it was he who had made them possible.

She was ready and waiting by one o'clock, and a good thing too, for he arrived half an hour early with all four children, explaining apologetically when she opened the door that they had insisted on coming with him to see where she lived. They each shook her by the hand and the little girls kissed her as well, and so, after a shy pause, did Hubert, but Dirk, although he greeted her politely, gave her an inimical look which momentarily chilled her, although the chill was dispelled at once by the professor's cheerful: 'Well, since we're all doing it…' and kissed her too. And although she hadn't been kissed all that number of times, it wasn't the lighthearted salute she occasionally received from William's friends, but quick and hard and disturbing. Of course, she told herself confusedly, he was an older man and would have had plenty of practice, and to dispel a vague dissatisfaction at the idea, she plunged into a lightning guided tour of the flat because the children were clamouring for it.

They were excited and also a little tired; the professor had driven down after his day's work on the previous evening and they had left Caundle Bubb quite early that morning, stopping for lunch on the way. They told her this, talking in chorus, telling her about Sugar and Beauty and that they were going to have a pony of their own at home now that they could ride a little; they told her that Mrs Burge had cried when they had left and that their father was coming home soon, and when they paused for breath: 'How nice to hear all your news,' cried Beth, just as though they hadn't seen each other for months instead of days. 'You shall tell me all over again presently, my dears, but now I think we should be going, don't you? Your mother will be wondering what has happened and your uncle mustn't be kept waiting.'

She smiled across the room at him and was surprised at his serious: 'But that is just what he is doing, Beth—waiting.'

'Oh, are you?' she exclaimed, rather bewildered. 'Then we had best go.'

She took a final look at the sitting-room, closed its door and led the party through the tiny hall and down the stairs, the professor last of all with her luggage. It took a few minutes to stow everyone comfortably while she greeted Mevrouw Thorbecke, and then they were off, the big car sliding with silent power through the shabby streets, making for the Dover road.

Beth had had no time to find out about the journey—indeed, looking back on the last two days, she wondered how she had managed to fit so much in; getting her visitor's passport, cleaning the flat and doing all that washing—and then the shopping; she should have been exhausted, but strangely enough she felt alive with excitement and full of energy; she didn't really care how they were going or how long it would take; the professor would have arranged everything admirably, she had no doubt. She sat back in the cramped back of the car and applied herself happily enough to answering the children's endless questions about anything which took their attention, which kept them all occupied until the professor stopped at Newingreen and they all piled out for tea at the Royal Oak.

It was a boisterous meal and eaten with no lack of appetite, and Beth, watching the professor stow away buttered toast, teacakes and buns with all the zest of his nephews, guessed that in all likelihood he had had nothing much the day before but a cup of coffee and stale sandwich from the hospital canteen—and not sufficient sleep either, she decided. Someone really ought to take him in hand.

But if he was tired, the professor didn't show it; they arrived at Dover, transferred themselves and the car without difficulty on to the Hovercraft and in due course arrived at Calais. Disembarking took a little time, but finally they were on the coast road, heading for Holland.

At De Panne the professor swept the car on to the road to Bruges, and when they reached that picturesque town went straight through it despite cries from the children, who wanted to stop and sightsee.

'Too late,' he told them good-naturedly. 'It'll be late enough by the time we get to Willemstad and your mother will be tired—and so will you. Another time.'

They tore on, circled Antwerp to reach the motorway to Breda and turned off again before they reached that city, to join a secondary road across pleasant wooded country. Beth, looking about her, liked it better than the motorway, which, while allowing one to travel at speed, which she liked, gave one little opportunity to see much. The children, on familiar ground now, were begging her to turn this way and that so that they might show well-remembered bits of scenery, becoming more and more excited with each kilometre, just as she was; she could hardly wait to see Willemstad. When they did reach it, it surprised her very much; she had expected quite a large town, instead of which, having passed some pleasant villas in their own gardens, they shot up a narrow street and came out quite unexpectedly by a small harbour. The road was cobbled and the houses lining it were old and charming to see. In the late spring sunshine the little place glimmered and shone as though it had been polished, and even as they looked the sun slid behind the horizon, leaving a soft not quite dark in which it was possible to distinguish a handful of fishing boats and some rather splendid yachts, and peering around

her, Beth could see a church, not a stone's throw from
the water, and what looked like the Town Hall, and
across the road from these ancient buildings, a rather
staid hotel. But she had little time to look around her,
for they had turned away from the harbour, between
an avenue of trees with shops on either side, and presently the professor turned the car carefully into a
narrow cobbled street with a high wall on one side and
a row of very small gabled cottages on the other. The
wall was pierced by a gate half-way down its length,
left open, presumably for them because he inched
through it and drew up before the door of the nice old
house only a few yards from it.

'Out you get,' he ordered genially, 'and get
indoors—take Beth with you. I'll bring your mother.'

There was a young woman at the open door, introduced as Maartje, and hovering somewhere at the back
of the hall was an older woman in an overall. 'That's
the cook,' explained Marineka. 'She's called Mies—
Maartje does the housework.' She tugged at Beth's
arm. 'Shall we go upstairs?'

Mevrouw Thorbecke had joined them and paused
in her greeting of Mies and Maartje to say: 'Yes,
Marineka, take Beth to her room—the one next to
yours, *liefje*.' She smiled at Beth. 'And welcome to my
home, Beth.'

Beth's room was charming. Both little girls had accompanied her and they were embarking on a happy

tour of inspection when their uncle's voice, requesting Beth's presence, interrupted them, so she went downstairs to the floor below, to Mevrouw Thorbecke's bedroom; a charming apartment containing everything any woman could wish for, although at the moment all Mevrouw Thorbecke wanted was her bed. Beth cast her a sympathetic look and set about the business of getting her out of her clothes and tucked up cosily against her pillows as quickly as possible, and that done, she tidied up, arranged a bedside lamp at a more convenient angle, fetched some magazines and announced her intention of bringing up supper.

'Thank you, Beth, how kind you are, but Maartje will be here in a moment with a tray—perhaps if you would see to the children? I feel very mean leaving you to see to everything like this…'

Beth smiled cheerfully. 'I'm not in the least tired,' she assured Mevrouw Thorbecke. 'I'll have a quick supper with them and get them off to bed, they must be tired out.'

They were in the dining room waiting for her; a large, rather formal room on the ground floor, with double doors leading to an even larger room which she supposed was the drawing room. The professor was there too, sitting in a carving chair, reading a paper, but he got up when she looked round the door and called: 'Yes, we're here, Miss Partridge, dying from hunger. Come and sit down at once and have a glass of something while Mies sends in the food.'

She sat, sipping a delicious Madeira which she feared might go to her head, and left him to finish his paper while she joined in the children's chatter, and presently they all fell to on the Sole Bonne Femme and followed that with a bread and butter pudding; a meal designed for the children, thought Beth, and very nice too, although she wondered if the professor found it quite to his taste. By now Alberdina was drooping over her plate, and regretfully refusing a second helping. Beth excused herself and the little girl and carried her off to bed, quickly followed by the other three. It was half an hour or more before they were finally settled in their rooms, for Alberdina refused to sleep until Pim the cat had been found and settled on the end of her bed, and then Beth had to be reminded by Hubert that Rufus, the golden retriever who had been at their heels since they arrived, was in the habit of sleeping in his basket in his room, and would she make sure that he did so before she went to bed herself.

Mevrouw Thorbecke was asleep by now and Beth went on downstairs; she had to discover what time breakfast was in the morning and what time the children got up. There was no one about; she opened and shut doors, beginning to feel a little like Alice, and was getting faintly annoyed when she was startled by the professor's voice. 'My dear girl, are you playing a game? You have been peering in and out of doors for the last two minutes.'

He spoke from above her and when she looked up she saw that he was leaning over the rail of the gallery above her head. He was laughing too and she said quite crossly: 'I can't find anyone and I'm getting quite demented, if you must know. There are all sorts of things I have to know and no one to tell me.'

He came downstairs with quiet speed. 'Ask me,' he invited.

'Well, at what time do I—and the children—get up? And when is breakfast? And is there any kind of routine to their day, and…'

'Let's ask Maartje,' he offered, and took her arm and opened the door leading to the kitchen at the end of the hall—a modern, gleaming kitchen in which Maartje and Mies were washing up. The professor spoke to them both and Beth could only guess at what he was saying, but they smiled and replied at some length, and finally he said: 'The children get up at half past seven and someone will call you then. Breakfast at half past eight, though when they go to school it's a good deal earlier. They go for a walk in the morning and I'm sure that by the time you're back, Martina will feel like telling you anything else you want to know.'

'Thank you,' Beth smiled at the two women and wished them good night as they went back to the hall, where she said: 'I'll go to bed too, I think. Are you staying here?'

He shook his head. 'No, I shall drive to my own home, just this side of Utrecht.'

'Is that where you work? William said something about Leyden…'

'I work there too sometimes, but mostly at Utrecht. Go to bed now, Elizabeth. I'll be over in a few days to see how you're getting on.'

Her face lit up. 'Oh, will you? That'll be super. Is it far to Utrecht?'

'No—just over an hour's run if you keep up a good speed. You shall come and see my home one day, dear girl.'

She glowed at the very idea. 'Oh, may I? I should like that, you see it's nice to know where you live and what your home's like and…' she stopped and went on lamely: 'When you remember people—when you think of them…'

'And will you think of me, Beth?'

She stared up at him, her pansy eyes wide. 'Oh, yes, more than I…' A look of utter shock crossed her face. 'Oh, I am a fool,' she said in a stunned little voice, and turned and ran for the stairs.

He caught her easily enough before she was even half-way up and without a word sat her down on a tread and lowered himself to sit beside her.

'Will you tell me, or shall I tell you?' he asked gently.

'No—' her voice was quiet too but rather high. 'Don't you see, if you don't talk about something, you can pretend it isn't true.' She made this childish remark without looking at him and so missed the tender amusement in his eyes; a smile which tugged at the corners of his mouth as well when she went on, with a fine disregard for what she had just said: 'I believe it happens a lot, this—this situation—at least, it does in books.'

The amusement was there, but he kept his voice placid. 'And you think that if we ignore this—er—situation, it will go away, as it were? Is that what you want, little Partridge?'

'Yes—and I wish you would not call me little Partridge in that way, it—it makes me feel...' She gave up the rest of what she was going to say, although her voice was still nice and steady, even though her awakened heart gave a sickening lurch at the very thought of him going out of her life for ever just when she had, as it were, discovered him. All the same, she would have to get things straight...'I've not been in love before,' she told him. 'Once or twice I thought I was, but that's quite different, isn't it? But I'm a sensible girl, you know, with no time to moon around, so there's—there's no harm done,' she swallowed bravely, 'and of course it's quite different for you—you must have loads of girlfriends; William has a different one every week.'

'William,' said the professor with some asperity, 'is a dozen years or more younger than I.'

'Oh, I know, but you're very good-looking and successful and a famous surgeon, and so—so nice. The girls at St Elmer's were quite turned on—you only had to lift a finger…'

'Contrary to your mistaken reading of my character, my girl, I am not in the habit of chatting up the birds.'

'Well, I don't suppose you have a great deal of time, do you?' she agreed soberly, unaware of his silent amusement. They sat without speaking for a few minutes; the professor seemed content to say nothing and Beth wanted only to go somewhere nice and quiet and have a good cry, but she was a tidy-minded girl and she wasn't sure that she had made herself quite clear. 'I think,' she began again, 'it would be best if we forgot this conversation, don't you?'

'I have a retentive memory,' interposed her companion meekly.

'Well, I can't help that,' she replied, nettled, 'and it can't be all that difficult for you; it isn't as if—that is, you don't really fancy me, do you? It's only because we've seen rather a lot of each other just lately and you've not seen any other girls. But we're not likely to see much of each other, are we, and I'm only here for a week or two.'

'You consider me quite unsuitable, little Partridge?'

'Not you—me, but you don't have to worry about that.'

'Ah, no. You are very sensible; you have already told me so.'

The trouble was that he was so very easy to talk to; she was pouring out her thoughts and feelings like water from a bucket when she should have hidden them behind a sudden headache or something. Instead of which she had actually let him see that she was in love with him. Well, if he had been surprised, so had she. She pulled herself together and said again: 'You must have any number of girls.'

The professor hid a smile. 'Oh, I have, Elizabeth, I have. Safety in numbers, so they say.'

'Well, then...' But she couldn't go on, her throat was thick with tears and there was really no need to say any more; she had made her point. It was quite a relief when the professor, not looking at her, said cheerfully: 'Go to bed, Beth. You have told me twice that you're a sensible girl and wish to forget this whole conversation, so let us do just that.' He got up and pulled her to her feet. 'Off with you!'

She flew upstairs, not looking back, because if she did she would have flown down again straight into his arms and suffered the bitter humiliation of knowing that he was being kind to her because he felt regret for something which had actually been no fault of his.

He hadn't encouraged her, she sobbed to herself as she got ready for bed, not once; he had been friendly and kind, and if she hadn't been such a little fool she would have known that she was falling in love with him and done something about it. Exactly what, she had no idea.

CHAPTER EIGHT

VIEWED in the early light of the morning, it was a nightmare; Beth went hot and cold just thinking about it. What must he have thought of her, letting him see so easily that she had fallen in love with him? True, she had done her best to put that right, hadn't she, but thinking about it, she wasn't sure if she had succeeded. But there was nothing to do about it now; she would have to stay until Mevrouw Thorbecke had found someone else or felt well enough to cope herself, because she had promised that she would, and if she kept out of his way it might not be too awful. The thought depressed her.

It was fortunate that the very nature of her work kept her so busy that she had very little leisure in which to ponder her situation. The children wouldn't be going back to school for another few weeks. Beth wasn't sure why; something to do with their father returning, she supposed, so in the meanwhile she controlled their natural exuberance to the best of her ability, taught them English; regular lessons in reading and writing each day, and accompanied them to the heated swimming pool at the bottom of the garden and, a little apprehensively, swam with them. They were all very good at it, even Alberdina, and Dirk, for one, made no secret of his scorn at her efforts to keep afloat. She found this a little hard to bear, but since their little adventure in the Cheddar Gorge, he had persistently cold-shouldered her, although he was always polite now; unnaturally so for a boy of ten, she considered— never smiling at her, never admitting her to the close friendship she enjoyed with the other children. She tried to be philosophical about it; children were as entitled to dislike people as grown-ups, only they had started out on such a good footing and she had no idea why it had gone wrong.

They went cycling too, and here she was able to hold her own with her charges, as they sped along the paths beside the main roads, with Dirk always in the lead, and herself bringing up the rear, with a hand on Alberdina's small shoulder to steady her on her own miniature bike.

And in the evenings, when the children were in bed, she sat with Mevrouw Thorbecke, talking about clothes or watching television, and sometimes, when Mevrouw Thorbecke was bored or depressed, Beth sat down at the grand piano in the enormous bay window of the sitting room and played little bits of anything that came into her head. She played rather well, and her companion, nicely soothed, would frequently confide her small worries to her. Beth listened silently, nodding her head from time to time and making soothing sounds as she played; she liked the other girl; they were as different as chalk from cheese and the professor's sister was undoubtedly spoiled and lazy, relying upon her husband for just about everything, and when he wasn't there, her brother, but she loved her children dearly and from what Beth could make out, adored her husband. It must be wonderful to be cherished like that, thought Beth, who hadn't been cherished for a very long time, and sighed as she brought her music to a halt and suggested a game of cards.

The professor came on Saturday morning, looking tired and driving a magnificent Aston Martin Lagonda. He suffered his small relations' rapturous greetings with calm, attended without fuss to several household matters which his sister assured him were pressing, nodded casually to Beth when he met her, and declared his intention of going sailing for the greater part of the day, and if the children wished to accompany him they were free to do so.

'That is if they have been good, Miss Partridge?' He smiled at her, his eyebrows lifted in casual, friendly inquiry. Above the excited shouts and squeals she assured him gravely that she had no fault to find with any of them, whereupon he crossed the room to where she was sitting, mending a doll for Alberdina.

'You will be glad of a few hours' peace and quiet,' he suggested, and she agreed composedly in a wooden voice which quite hid her true feelings. Of course, it would have been absurd of him to suggest that she might have liked to go too. She felt unaccountable annoyance because he hadn't, forgetful of her resolve to see as little of him as possible.

She helped the children prepare for their treat, went to the kitchen to ask, in her fragmented Dutch, that a picnic might be prepared, and went back upstairs until the children were ready. She didn't go downstairs with them; Mevrouw Thorbecke was at the door, waiting to see the party off and there was no need for her to go. The children raced down the stairs, shouting their good-byes as they went, but Alberdina came trotting back to throw her arms round her neck and wish that she was coming too. Beth, much touched, kissed the round cheek, assured her that she would be waiting to hear all about their day when they returned, and sent her running after the others.

Mevrouw Thorbecke had seconded her brother's suggestion that Beth should have the rest of the day free until the sailing party returned. She excused herself from lunch, took her writing things and wandered off, taking care to walk away from the harbour in case she should be seen by the children. But after half an hour, when she judged they should be gone, she wended her way back through the little town and strolled round its small harbour, watching the *boeier*, already quite a way out, fast disappearing into the distance. As she turned away, she wondered if the professor had a yacht of his own; it would be exceptional if he hadn't, for he seemed to have everything.

She had coffee and a *kaas broodje* in the hotel, and since it was perfect sailing weather and everyone who had the chance was on the water, the place was almost empty. She had a second cup of coffee, and began a letter to William. But she couldn't think of much to write about; she touched on the perfect weather, the pleasant little town, the children and the vague possibility of her return within a short time, hoped that he was coping with the housekeeping and ended this rather dull missive with various instructions regarding the shopping and his laundry. She then took herself off to post it, and because there was really nothing more to do, she went back to the house, collected some knitting from her room and went out into the garden, where she sat doing nothing at all until the commotion made by the returning sailors roused her from her thoughts.

Beth looked at her watch; it was after five o'clock. She hadn't gone in for a cup of tea at half past three because she had heard a car full of visitors arriving, and if Mevrouw Thorbecke had friends to tea it would be better if she didn't join them, because then everyone was forced to speak English, which might have been rather a bore for them. She got up now, carefully packed up the knitting she hadn't touched, and went indoors to where the children, very excited, were telling their mother about their day, while their uncle lounged in a chair, his eyes shut.

Mevrouw Thorbecke gave a relieved sigh as Beth entered the room.

'Ah, Beth, there you are! I have a headache—all those wretched people calling and talking like magpies—would it not be a good idea if the children were to have their tea in the playroom with you? Then they could have their baths and be ready for dinner. There must be some quiet game they could play then.'

Beth agreed quickly, conscious of the professor's eyes, open now, upon her, and torn between relief at not having to talk to him and disappointment at not seeing him again until dinner, she led the children away, still talking at the tops of their voices, except for Dirk, of course, who answered her questions civilly enough, but volunteered no remarks of his own. But the other children made up for his silence; they talked and giggled themselves through an enormous tea and then settled down to a game of Monopoly behind closed doors because of the noise, shrieking with laughter at Beth's endeavours to play in a foreign language, until it was time for their baths.

It was striking eight when she led them downstairs, the elder three very clean and smart because their uncle would be there, and Alberdina in her dressing-gown, ready for bed. And as for Beth, she had put on the purple dress and made up her face in a very perfunctory fashion, dragging her hair back with a severity which somehow made her look very young indeed.

Dinner was eaten with a good deal of laughter and talking and small sleepy giggles from Alberdina, whom Beth whisked away as soon as the last of her pudding had been spooned up, returning to escort Hubert to his bed and then go down once more to drink her coffee in the drawing room while Dirk and Marineka, being the two eldest, were enjoying another fifteen minutes with the grown-ups. They, in their turn, said good night, and she got up with them, adding her own good nights.

'Mr dear good girl,' expostulated the professor, 'you can't possibly go to bed at nine o'clock. Besides, I want to talk to you.'

He had said he would forget their regrettable conversation on the stairs, and it seemed he had; Beth told herself she should be glad as she agreed to join them again, but only because Mevrouw Thorbecke had added her voice to her brother's.

They were going to tell her that she could return to St Elmer's, she decided, but it wasn't that at all. The professor offered her a chair opposite his sister, seated himself where he could look at her and stated simply: 'You have had no day off, Beth. I should like to drive you to my home tomorrow.'

She glanced at him, sitting back at his ease, elegant in his tweeds, and encountered a smile to charm the heart out of her. 'Martina agrees with me.'

'It's very kind of you,' she paused to steady her breath, 'but I'm quite happy with the children, you know.'

'You would rather not come out with me?' asked the professor unfairly, seeing that his sister was listening to every word.

'Nothing of the sort,' she assured him, her colour a little high, 'only it seemed to me that it wouldn't be a very restful day for you—you looked tired when you arrived this morning; surely a day doing nothing would do you much more good?'

He was amused behind his placid face. 'What sharp eyes you have, Miss Partridge—no one else saw that. Perhaps you might change your mind if I tell you that I can think of no pleasanter way of spending my day than showing you my home.' He smiled again. 'Ten o'clock?' he suggested.

Short of saying no, which would have sounded ungracious and very rude, she could do nothing else but accept gracefully.

It was a splendid opportunity to wear the new dress and Beth, surveying herself in the mirror the next morning, thought, quite erroneously, that its demure grey was most suitable; the type of dress which would pass unnoticed without being dowdy. In fact it emphasized her remarkable eyes to a degree which would have satisfied any girl with an ounce of conceit; but conceit was something Beth had never had; her step-brother had seen to that.

It took a little while to explain her dressed-up person to the children at breakfast, a meal taken in the playroom; she had barely finished reassuring Alberdina and Hubert that she really would be coming back that day when a cheerful bellow from the profes-sor sent her down to the hall where he and his sister were waiting.

'That's a pretty dress,' observed the professor, and added: 'Good morning, Elizabeth.'

She wished them both a good day, replied suitably to Mevrouw Thorbecke's observance that it was a lovely morning, and accompanied the professor out to his car, with the children swarming around them, the little girls to kiss her good-bye just once more and the boys to stare at the magnificence of the Aston Martin and start on a spate of questions, cut short by their uncle with a: 'We're off—out of the way, my dears—*tot ziens*.'

They went down the short drive to the accompani-ment of shouted good-byes and a forest of waving arms. 'A royal send-off,' commented the professor. 'Anyone might think that we were off on our honeymoon.'

Unanswerable. 'A lovely day,' Beth observed, wishing that they were.

'So Martina has already said, though she was referring to the weather; I hope you mean something different, little Partridge.'

'It's very nice to be going out,' said Beth woodenly, and added, in a praiseworthy attempt at normal conversation: 'I'm not sure where you live—is it in Utrecht?'

'No, I work there most of the time, I told you that, I believe. My home is in a very small village indeed, much smaller than Caundle Bubb, and that's small enough, isn't it? It's six miles from Utrecht and is called Dwaarstein. We go over the Moerdijk to get to it...' He talked on, mainly about the country they were passing through, so that presently Beth relaxed and began to enjoy herself.

They stopped in Dordrecht for coffee, at a pleasant restaurant in the centre of the town, and although her companion offered to spend a little time there if she wished, she sensed that he wanted to get on; and so did she; she wanted to see his home very badly, and still more, she wanted to know more about him although she was sensible enough to know that this was a foolish wish; the less she knew about him the better. But common sense was eclipsed for the moment. She sat beside him, obediently looking at anything he pointed out to her, and peeping, from time to time, at him. When he wasn't looking, of course.

They were tearing along the motorway again, going through pleasant, flat country, prettily wooded here and there, and from discussing the scenery, the professor had turned the conversation, almost unnoticed, to more personal matters. It was only after Beth had told him her rather vague plans for the future that she realized that she was gabbing about herself, and stopped so abruptly that he gave her a quick glance, slowed the car, and asked: 'A new bee in your bonnet, Beth?'

'What do you mean—a new bee?'

'Well, I have already discovered several, you know. You have one about your quite charming face, have you not? And one about seeing that William gets his chance in life, even at the cost of your own wishes—I wonder how many new dresses you have forgone in order to keep up his supply of waistcoats? And you have one, a very large one, about the unsuitability of an English nurse falling in love with a Dutch professor.' He ignored her gasp. 'And now, unless I am very much mistaken, I am faced with yet another—a mistaken idea that I must be told nothing of your plans for the future. I can't think why.' He sighed. 'Pride, I daresay.'

'Don't be ridiculous,' she snapped, taking refuge in bad temper. 'And I thought that we were never going to mention...'

'Ah, yes—my lamentable memory.'

'But you said you had a very retentive brain...'

'True, but only when I want it to be.' He swung the car off the motorway and under a flyover and emerged on to the other side, on a much narrower country road. 'We're almost there—Utrecht is away to our right, about twelve miles away. I can reach it from Dwaarstein by another road.'

He turned off again, down a pretty, tree-lined avenue, curving this way and that for no reason but to allow for several charming villas to be set in its curves. Half-way down it the professor turned once more, this time through an open gateway with pillars on either side of it, running more slowly now, between the trees and shrubs of a small wood. It wasn't until they were almost at its end that Beth could see the house, set a little to one side of a gravel sweep. It was large and square, with rows of large windows and a wide door reached by double steps. The professor drew up, got out and came round to open her door with an economy of movement which drew her admiration. So many men fussed around, kicking tyres and trying door handles, going back to peer inside; he was one of the few men she had met who just got into a car and drove away, and when he arrived, he got out again without loss of time and no fuss at all. He was an excellent driver, but he was excellent at everything... She dragged her thoughts back to the present and looked about her.

'Well?' asked her companion with a touch of impatience.

'It's beautiful,' she told him, and meant it. 'It looks so solid and safe and although it's large it looks like a home...' She had forgotten him for a moment. 'In the winter, with lights in all the windows and children running about...' She stopped, feeling silly. 'I'm sorry, I was just daydreaming.'

He took her arm. 'I do the same thing myself,' he assured her cheerfully. 'Come inside.'

There was an elderly man to open the door for them, and he reminded her of someone. 'This is Silver,' said the professor, 'Mrs Silver's brother. He married a Dutch girl and settled down here—he and Ria run the place for me. I don't know what I should do without them.'

Silver smiled benignly, acknowledged Beth's greeting with a dignified inclination of his balding head and ushered them into the hall, where they were instantly set upon by the two dogs, Gem and Mini, uttering little barks of pleasure while they allowed Beth to rub their ears and stroke their well-groomed coats before accompanying them across the hall, a roomy place, carpeted in crimson and housing a selection of fine antique furniture under a massive crystal chandelier, to a pair of doors which Silver flung open with something of a flourish, to reveal a room of great magnificence, furnished in muted colours which served to highlight the rose velvet curtains draping the floor-length windows and with an immense hooded fireplace with a tiled surround. The walls were hung with painted leather and the carpet on the parquet floor was an enormous Aubusson reflecting the rose colour of the curtains; its furniture was a cunning mixture of comfort and antiques.

'Oh,' said Beth, 'how very grand—I mean, I didn't expect it, you know. I thought you would have a nice house, because the houses in England are quite beautiful—but this house is different.'

'Old.' The professor spoke briefly. 'It's been in the family for a very long time, and of course we don't see anything very unusual about it. I was born here and I've lived here, on and off, all my life. It's home to me.'

She blinked her pansy eyes at him. 'Oh, I know—don't think I don't like it, I think it's absolutely super—what I meant was that you don't look like a person who lives so grandly.' She caught his eyes and smiled doubtfully. 'Have I made you angry? I explained clumsily.'

He burst out laughing. 'Why should I be angry, dear girl? That's the very last feeling you engender in me.' He turned his head as the door opened and a tall, thin woman came in. 'Ah, Ria, there you are. Beth, this is Silver's wife, Ria. She will take you upstairs. I'll be here when you come down.'

She followed the housekeeper up the carved oak staircase which opened out on to a long gallery and Ria opened one of the doors in it and smilingly invited her to enter. The room was large too, probably all the rooms were, thought Beth, going to look out of the window which looked out on to a well-tended garden of some size, glowing with spring flowers and thickly fringed by trees. The two dogs ran across the grass as she looked, and there was a tabby cat curled up on a garden seat. She sighed unconsciously and took a look at herself in the great oval mirror above the bow-fronted table and in one corner of the room, and, dissatisfied with what she saw, pinned her hair back even more severely and resumed her inspection of the room.

It was furnished daintily with a canopied bed, a tall-boy of rosewood, some comfortable chairs and a table or two, and the curtains and hangings were a pleasing combination of pale silks and chintz. There was a very modern bathroom too, concealed behind a little door in one wall, and yet another door led back into the gallery. Beth picked up her handbag and went downstairs, walking slowly, trailing a hand on the polished rail as she went.

The professor was where she had left him, contemplating the garden. He turned to look at her as she went in. 'You've been at your hair again,' he said at once. 'Why do you drag it back so cruelly? Such lovely hair too.'

She looked at him helplessly. 'I…!' she began, not knowing in the least what she was going to say. She had armed herself against his charm, or so she had thought. She had determined to forget the regrettable episode on the stairs, she had made up her mind to get through the next week or so without allowing herself the luxury of thinking of him in any way but as someone she liked and wasn't likely to meet again, and here she was, within ten minutes of being in his house, tonguetied. If only he wouldn't be so kind! She had no wish to be pitied; it was bad enough that he had guessed her feelings for him before she had discovered them for herself. She frowned quite fiercely and looked away from him.

'Did anyone tell you that your face betrays every thought in that head of yours?' he wanted to know, and crossed the room. 'Or is it that I can read them so well?'

'I expect,' said Beth carefully, 'that you get very clever at that—being a surgeon.'

'I'm a man as well,' he reminded her, and to make that quite clear, bent to kiss her.

She kissed him back; as well be hanged for a sheep as for a lamb, and just for a minute he held her close, looking down into her face.

'Why, I do believe you've got rid of the bees,' he declared softly.

'Not really—I—I just got carried away.' It was ridiculous how she could say such things to him and feel no awkwardness at all; it was like talking to herself and far more satisfactory. 'It's a funny thing,' she went on thoughtfully, 'I should feel awful talking to you like this, shouldn't I, and I don't. I think I have no pride after all.'

He loosed her and took her arm and started walking towards the door.

'Oh, but you have: "Trust thou thy love; if she be proud, is she not sweet?" That's your Ruskin describing you to a T.'

Beth had the sensation of running downhill very fast. She didn't look at him. 'I don't understand...'

'You are very sweet, Beth—you're proud too.' He opened the door. 'Shall we look round the garden before we have lunch?'

It was silly to feel so disappointed, for what in heaven's name had she expected him to say? That was the worst of daydreaming, it made one foolish. She swallowed her mortified feelings and said: 'I should like that very much,' and stepped out into the sunshine with him.

The gardens were lovely; they wandered up and down the paths, stopping to admire and examine and discuss the magnificent show of spring flowers. Beth was surprised when her companion admitted to a liking for pottering amongst his flower beds. 'It's restful,' he explained, 'and when I want to have a quiet think I do it better out of doors.'

'Oh—you don't look that kind of man at all.'

He stopped to look at her. 'No? What kind of man do you think I am, Beth? Did I not tell you that I wasn't one to chat up the birds?'

She hastened to agree with him. 'Oh, I'm sure you're not, but you must go out a good deal,' she waved a hand towards the house before them. 'All this...you must have loads of friends and entertain them sometimes.'

He grinned and she went pink. 'What you want to know is whom do I entertain, isn't it, dear girl? Set your mind at rest, I'm a very ordinary man, possessed at the moment with a lively desire to marry the girl I love and settle down.' He put out a hand and started to take the pins out of her hair, so that it hung around her shoulders. When he had finished he handed them to her. 'That's better, now you're beautiful.' He smiled a little. 'There is so much I want to say to you, Beth, but I dare not, not just yet, for if I did you would imagine that I was saying it because of that conversation on the stairs which I'm not allowed to remember—and there has to be no doubt in your mind. Do you find me too old?'

She was so surprised that she could only gape at him. 'Old?' she managed. 'You're not even middle-aged…'

He kissed her again, very gently on her cheek. 'Good, then from this moment, Beth, will you stop thinking of me as a professor of surgery with more money than is good for him, and call me Alexander and remind yourself every few minutes that we are going to be something more than good friends? We have to begin somewhere, you know.'

Her head swam with the oddest mixture of thoughts, but it was no good trying to sort them out now. She said: 'Yes, Alexander,' in a meek voice, only too glad that someone else was making up her mind for her. It was rather an anticlimax when he said cheerfully: 'Lunch, I think,' and strolled with her into the house, talking about the roses on the south wall, just as though he hadn't said a single one of the exciting words tumbling round inside her head.

They lunched in a room large enough to accommodate with ease the massive round table in its centre, with its matching chairs; an enormous sideboard upon whose polished surface was a splendid display of silver, and another hooded fireplace.

'Dreadfully old-fashioned,' remarked the professor as they sat down, 'but I'm old-fashioned myself—how does it strike you?'

Beth gazed about her. 'But it's just right. I wonder who thought of those little wall chandeliers and that gorgeous crimson wallpaper? They're perfect!'

He leaned back in his carving chair, looking smug. 'How could anyone help but like you, dear girl—you always say the right thing at the right time. I did.'

He talked about the house and its history while they enjoyed a delicious ratatouille followed by fillet steak, flavoured with mushrooms, garlic and some sort of sausage, and it had undoubtedly been cooked in wine. Beth would have liked to ask but felt too shy, and even if she did, she wasn't sure if the professor, while appreciating good food, bothered himself much as to how it had been cooked. She allowed him to re-fill her glass with the Chianti they were drinking, and daintily polished off the crêpes soufflés au citron which Silver had placed before her, while she listened to her host's quiet voice talking with affection about his home. The wine had relaxed her by now, and she felt incapable of worrying about anything at all—it was sufficient to enjoy the moment.

They went back to the drawing room for their coffee, before spending some time in the long gallery running across the back of the house, its windows looking out on to the garden, its inner wall hung with a number of paintings, some of them a little dark and forbidding, but most of them charming family groups of sober gentlemen in a variety of bygone costumes, standing guard over their wives and children.

'Were any of them doctors or surgeons?' she wanted to know.

'Lord, yes. There's always been someone—mostly surgery.' He opened a little painted door at the end of the gallery and ushered her into a small corner room with windows on two sides, cosily furnished with chintz-covered chairs and a number of small tables and cabinets.

'My mother always sat here to do her accounts,' he said. 'I don't come here often—it's a large house. Unless I have guests, I never seem to get further than my study and the dining room.'

His words conjured up a lonely life; Beth was on the point of saying so when she stopped; it would be treading on thin ice again. That she loved him was an unchangeable fact, and he had let her see that he was attracted to her, perhaps loved her a little. But how much? she wondered. He might think he was, but it might not last; her good sense told her that what to her was serious might be to him a pleasant romantic episode and nothing more. She remarked on the charming work table by the side of the fireplace and kept the conversation firmly on antiques for the rest of her visit.

They drove back to Willemstad after tea, with Beth almost at the end of topics of an impersonal nature to talk about and the professor silently amused and placid. They were half-way down the lane leading to his sister's house when he drew up, switched off the engine and turned to her.

He said gently: 'It's silly to be scared, Beth. It would be so very easy for me to convince you that your fears are non-existent—but I won't, not just yet.'

She looked at her hands resting quietly in her lap. 'I'm not scared, truly I'm not—it's difficult to explain, but you see I'm so ordinary. If I were pretty or had loads of money or had done something quite extraordinary, it would seem more—more likely, but I'm not any of these things. I can't imagine what you see in me, and it might not last, that's if you do...'

'Love you? I'll tell you about that next time we see each other.' He started the car again and without another word went into the house again, to be instantly surrounded by the children. He left an hour later, calling good-bye to her in a casual way and without saying when they would meet again.

CHAPTER NINE

BETH spent a wakeful night, alternating between despair and wild happiness. By the morning she knew that when the professor came, and if he asked her, she was going to tell him that she would marry him. He hadn't actually told her that he loved her, but that, she realized now, was because she hadn't given him the chance. She got out of bed and looked out of the window. It was going to be another lovely spring day, although there was a line of woolly clouds tucked into the horizon, probably early morning cloud. She put on her slacks and a cotton shirt and went to see if the children were getting up.

Mevrouw Thorbecke had a headache and had decided to stay in bed until lunchtime, so after breakfast Beth proposed a cycle ride to the children and an English lesson to follow and then went along to Mevrouw Thorbecke's room to see if there was anything she could do for her. There wasn't much; a little pillow shaking, the finding of some headache tablets, and some eau-de-cologne and a few instructions for Mies. Beth drew the brocade curtains closed and went along to the kitchen, where she and Mies engaged themselves in conversation at which they had become expert; signs and nods and an odd word here and there. They parted amicably ten minutes later and Beth went in search of the children.

They were nowhere to be found; she looked through the house, searched the garden and then went to see if the bicycles had gone. They hadn't; she sighed with relief and went down the lane and into the street.

They were up to some lark of their own, probably in a shop, and they couldn't be far away. Besides, four children could scarcely walk through the little town without being seen. She tried several shops without success until the greengrocer pointed towards the harbour, talking volubly as he did so. She thanked him, not having understood a word, but knowing what he meant, and crossed the road by the Stadhuis, to stand, looking left and right. They were at the far end of the harbour, by the harbour-master's house; she could see Marineka's red jersey. She heaved a sigh of relief and started to walk around the curve of water, to be stopped after a few yards by the *dominee*, wanting to know, in his careful, slow English, how Mevrouw Thorbecke did and if she herself was in good health. He was a nice old man. Beth answered his questions without haste and managed not to look over her shoulder to see what the children were up to. They talked for quite five minutes before she said goodbye and started off once more. The children weren't there—and to make matters worse there were small clouds sliding across the sky to hide the sun and dim her view. There were a great many yachts moored in the harbour and a forest of masts between her and the harbour mouth, but it was actually no distance and they were probably hiding because they had seen her. She reached the harbourmaster's house and went round the patch in front of it, so that now she could see the small stretch of enclosed water and the open lock which led to the Hollandsche Diep. The children were there all right, in the *boeier*, with its sails spread, already a little way from the shore. Beth closed her eyes for a second, then took a calming breath before calling cheerfully: 'Hi there—what about coming back before the rain starts?'

It was Dirk who answered. 'We're not going to— we're going for a sail. I know all about it and we don't want you—you can go home and wait for us, and I don't care if you do sneak!' He sounded defiant.

'What in the world should I sneak for? Come on back, Dirk, I'm sure you're a first class sailor, but I think it would be a good idea if you brought the others back.'

He didn't answer, and Beth saw the boat, caught in a sudden gust of wind, driving further away from the shore. They would be through the lock in no time at all and out into open water. And not only that, the wind was freshening fast and the little clouds were all of a sudden big ones. She walked along the edge of the water, using all her persuasive powers with absolutely no effect. It was when she heard Alberdina's small voice wailing that she slithered down the bank, took off her shoes, slid into the water and began to swim laboriously towards the *boeier*.

She hadn't really stopped to think, which was just as well, for she was terrified and she had no illusions about her swimming, but although she didn't know it, the strong current helped her, sweeping her along until she reached the boat, which was bowing merrily along now with only a few yards to go before it went through the narrow opening which would send it into the Hollandsche Diep. Somehow she scrambled on board, with Marineka and Hubert helping her and laughing at the same time. For them, she thought sourly, it was a fine joke, but for her it had been a wit-scaring experience she vowed she would never repeat, and now here she was, sitting on the deck of a boat she hadn't the faintest idea how to sail and wringing wet into the bargain. But it would never do to let them see how angry she was. She said between chattering teeth: 'Heavens, I had no idea I could swim so well! And now what about getting back, so I can get out of these wet things?'

It was too late. As she spoke the *boeier*, caught by another, stronger gust of wind, plunged ahead, its sails billowing, sturdily ploughing through water which had become quite alarmingly rough, and Marineka, who had gone back to the tiller, suddenly left it again, declaring that it was too heavy for her and that she was frightened. Beth had only the haziest notion of what sailing entailed, but she did know that someone had to steer; she took the little girl's place and called to Dirk, busy in the curved bows of the boat: 'How do we turn round?'

He turned a frightened little boy's face to her and she saw with a sinking heart that his boasting hadn't meant a thing, he didn't know much more than she did. He said now: 'I don't know, Beth. I think we have to take in sail. There is a wind—sometimes there are sudden storms and it is dangerous...'

He was right; the sky was a uniform grey now, pressing low on their heads, and the wind, no longer just gusts of it, was blowing steadily, taking them further and further away from land.

'Well, what shall we do?' asked Beth, carefully keeping panic out of her voice. 'Shall I leave this thing and come and help you or stay where I am?'

'You cannot leave the tiller—I will try and get the sails down, but there are knots...'

'But oughtn't we to keep at least one sail up, or we shall drift—isn't it called running before the wind?' She was hopelessly vague about what to do next, but she remembered having read that somewhere and now the wind was too strong for them to do anything else.

'Shall we try and reach the shore—there's land on either side of us,' she peered through the fine rain which was beginning to fall. 'It's a long way off,' she couldn't help adding: 'Shall we try the left or the right?'

They decided on the left, but the wind was too strong for them. The boat, broad and steady, was safe enough, she thought, but it needed more than herself and Dirk to manage it, and the other children were too frightened to be of much help. They might have a better chance if they went straight ahead; there would be land somewhere ahead of them. She tried to remember what Holland looked like; there were a number of islands, she knew that, divided by a great number of waterways leading to the North Sea. She wrinkled her brows, trying to remember what the professor had told her about them—there were dykes, enormous ones, enclosing some of the islands, and there was a bridge, but that was further south. They would have to keep on; they were bound to reach something sooner or later—sooner, she prayed fervently.

The boat had a roomy, well equipped cabin; she sent the three younger children down below and told Marineka to wrap themselves up in blankets if there were any. 'And I'll be down in a few minutes,' she promised.

Dirk had given up messing about with the sails; Beth called to him to take her place and followed the children to the cabin, where she settled them as comfortably as possible, found some lemonade and biscuits, then took off her wet shirt and pulled on a vast knitted garment in one of the lockers. She took the second one back with her and made Dirk put it on, then sent him below to have his share of the food. By the time he joined her the rain had blotted out the land and she asked him:

'Where are we, Dirk?'

He gave her a sullen look. 'I don't know—at least, we're in the Grevelingen Krammer. Oost Flakkee is on that side, but there aren't any harbours for miles.'

He sounded near to tears, despite the sullen looks, so she said cheerfully:

'Then we'd best keep on, hadn't we?'

Now that she was getting over her fright, she looked around to see if there was anything she could understand in the boat—yachts had automatic steering wheels and things like that, and the *boeier*, although it had been adapted from a fishing boat's shape, was nevertheless a kind of yacht. And surely it wasn't as difficult as all that to get a sail down? But even if they succeeded in this, supposing the wind dropped, how would they get it up again? However did people manage? thought Beth desperately and then said aloud: 'An engine—there has to be an engine. Dirk, where is it?'

He pointed to a wooden cover on the deck and shrugged his shoulders. 'It's there, but I don't know how it works.'

'Then I'll get it going.' She raised her voice above

the wind. It must be a gale by now, she thought worriedly. She had no idea how fast they were sailing now, but at the rate they were travelling, it couldn't be long before they reached somewhere. A sudden picture, making her feel quite sick, of them being blown into the North Sea before she could do anything about it sent her cautiously along the deck to the wooden cover, which, after two or three attempts, she managed to open.

She had no idea what kind of engine it might be— not that it would have helped much if she had known; it looked a jumble of machinery which remained stubbornly silent when she tried one or two experimental pokes, but it had to go if only she knew how. She replaced the cover and went back to Dirk at the tiller. 'There must be a chart or something of the sort,' she told him. 'I'm going to have a look for one.'

In the cabin the children were curled up together. Beth paused to tell them that they were almost at their journey's end—a fictitious piece of nonsense which they believed—and started her search. She found what she was looking for quite quickly and took it triumphantly back to Dirk.

'I'll take the tiller,' she told him, 'and you have a look at it for me.'

To her relief he understood at least some of it. All the same it took a very long time before, between them, they had puzzled it out and even then she was a little scared to try it. But she had to, for the storm was worsening all the time and she had the nasty feeling that the mistlike rain would make it difficult for anyone to see them from the shore. She took off the cover once more, and began to poke around. Nothing happened; she knelt on the deck, holding on to the rail with both hands, and fought a desire to burst into tears. If only Alexander were there! He would have known what to do and would have done it without fuss, and by now they would all have been home and dry—and safe. The nightmare trip had lasted for hours; they must have come miles and there was nothing to be seen. Even as she thought it, she saw land looming out of the greyness ahead of them. She flung herself down beside Dirk, shouting urgently above the gale: 'Dirk, that's land—can't we stop? Where is it?'

'It's the new dyke, I think, but I don't think we can stop—the wind's blowing us through that opening— we'll have to go on.'

'But we must, Dirk—it's our chance. Let's just try.'

It was hopeless and dangerous besides; the *boeier*, tough though she was, shuddered alarmingly when they altered course, caught in a cross-wind which almost turned her over. With the strength of fear, they got her back on course again and slid through the gap, the dyke behind them now, and a waste of grey water ahead.

'I'm going to have another go,' said Beth fiercely. And this time she was lucky; she hadn't the slightest idea how she had done it, but the motor coughed, sighed, coughed again and came alive. She stayed by it for a minute, hardly believing her ears, then shouted: 'Dirk—it's going! Now we can turn, can't we?'

He stared at her from a white face. 'Uncle Alexander said never—we have to alter course very slowly at intervals.'

It sounded awful. She shuddered at the risks they were taking and pulled herself together. 'What comes after that dyke?'

'There's Schouwen Duiveland that way—I think we're nearer there than anywhere else. There's a place called Brouwershaven—a harbour.'

She said resolutely: 'OK, we'll go there. Would you recognize it?'

He thought about it. 'I think perhaps—I'm not sure; I sailed this way with my father, but it was a long time ago—it's a long way.'

'You can say that again, but at least we know where we're going.' She gave him an encouraging smile. 'I'm going to see how the others are.'

Incredibly, they were sleeping, worn out with fright and excitement. Beth collected some more biscuits and took them back to Dirk and huddled beside him again. She wasn't frightened any more; the storm was just as fierce as ever and she had no idea how they would be able to sail into a harbour without coming to grief; she didn't know how to stop the engine and neither of them knew how to get the sails down; all the same, she wasn't scared. She munched a biscuit and thought about the professor.

She had lost all count of time when Dirk shouted: 'There is the little island, and the dyke they were building—we have to go round that point of land you can just see.'

'Good—do you think we could turn a little? I can't see any harbour, though, is it hidden?'

'It faces the other way.' He gave her a scared look. 'It will be difficult.'

The understatement of the year! All the same she said briskly: 'Alter course, Dirk, we're almost at the point.'

The harbour entrance was so narrow that they almost missed it, and for a few moments Beth thought that the stout little boat would be blown past it. Desperately she made her way to the motor and turned all the levers she could see. The diesel, more by good luck than anything else, stopped and in the nick of time the *boeier*, with billowing sails, swept into the harbour. But they were going much too fast; she could see the little town, built tidily on either side of the harbour which ran into its heart, and alarmingly close. They would have to stop, but after coming all that way, the idea of bumping into one of the yachts berthed on either side of them was unthinkable. She clawed her way to the mast and pulled and tugged, not knowing what she was doing, but to such good effect that the sails came hurtling down in a great untidy heap and they floundered to a stop, close enough to a stout motor cruiser so that she could lean over the side and hang on while Dirk made fast. It wasn't perhaps quite the way to berth, but it would serve—and they were going to get help; they had stopped exactly in front of the police station, an impressive building which spelled security and safety and perhaps a hot drink. There was a large policeman, wrapped in oilskins, crossing the cobbles, to come to a halt on the harbour side and shout down to them. Dirk answered him at some length and the man jumped down, made the boat fast with seamanlike expertise, grinned at Beth and went below to the children. He carried Alberdina up on deck while Beth collected Hubert and Marineka, spoke to Dirk again, and led the way over to the police station, where he ushered them into a waiting room and went to fetch someone else—a more senior man, Beth surmised, who, heaven be praised, spoke English. Before she had finished telling him what had happened, the first man was back again with a tray of hot coffee and thick slices of bread and cheese. Swallowing the scalding drink, she thought she had never tasted anything so good. 'If the children could be got warm?' she asked, 'and could we telephone their mother?'

'At once, miss.' The two men smiled at her in a fatherly way. 'Would you wish to speak, or shall we do it for you? It is perhaps not good that the children talk to their mother. They are tired…'

'Well, if you wouldn't mind—if you could explain. I can't speak Dutch and although Mevrouw Thorbecke speaks English, it would be easier…'

The older man nodded. 'I go now,' he assured her. 'There is a stove in the other room, if you will take the children there and ask for anything you would wish for.'

It was so cosily safe she could have gone to sleep there and then, but first the children had to be dried and warmed and cuddled a little. She turned from rubbing Alberdina's small icy feet to find the policeman back again. 'There was a Professor van Zeust on the telephone,' he told her, 'these children's uncle, is it not? I have told him all, and he comes to fetch you back to Willemstad.' He paused, looking at her. 'I warn you that he is exceedingly angry, miss. He said—his words— "the stupid, idiotic little fool, I could kill her!"' He shrugged enormous shoulders. 'He does not mean that, of course—naturally, he was worried, and when a man is worried he says such things. Now you will all have more coffee, for you, miss, do not look well. It is perhaps the shock of sailing the *boeier* through such a bad storm.'

Beth wanted to tell him that she hadn't sailed it; she hadn't known how, but it would be a waste of time and only lead to a lot more questions—time enough to explain when Alexander arrived. Perhaps by the time he did, he would have got over his anger.

She saw the Citroën tearing along the road on the other side of the harbour long before the others did. It disappeared from sight for a few moments and then snapped into view, to stop dead in front of the police station, and all her worst fears were realized. The professor wasn't just angry, he was in a white hot rage, all the more frightening because of the calm of his face. He strode in, made himself known to the Commandant, answered the children's cries of delight in a warm, perfectly normal voice, and gave her a look of such bottled-up fury that she quailed. It was only after a short conversation with the two policemen, and the briefest of colloquies with Dirk, that he spoke to her. They were leaving the building, the three elder children in front, Alberdina between them, when he said in a low, furious voice: 'You little idiot, Elizabeth, endangering all your lives in a such a foolhardy fashion! What was your purpose—what did you hope to gain from such a hare-brained scheme? And why tell Dirk that you could handle a boat and persuade him…'

She could think of nothing to say and she couldn't take refuge behind a ten-year-old boy, even though he was wholly to blame. She looked stonily ahead of her and didn't say a word, and neither, after his outburst, did the professor. She sat in the back of the car, with Alberdina on her lap and the other two beside her, half asleep now, and Dirk sat with his uncle, talking earnestly. The professor drove very fast, his temper once more under control, talking very little; mostly questions to Dirk. Only as they reached Willemstad did he say to them all: 'Your mother has been very frightened. You are to be good and quiet, all of you, and do exactly as you are told, and you must all be very tired and hungry. Supper and bed, I think, and you can tell her all about it in the morning.'

He led the way into the old house, calling out something Beth couldn't understand in a cheerful voice, and Martina Thorbecke came running down the stairs, laughing and crying and trying to embrace all four of her children at once. But presently she asked questions, answered briefly by her brother, and then, at great length, by Dirk, and when the professor would have hushed the boy, his mother shook her head and bade him go on, and Beth, standing quietly behind the others, saw the look Mevrouw Thorbecke shot at her and wondered what Dirk was saying.

Only when Maartje appeared and took the children away with her did Mevrouw Thorbecke speak to Beth. 'What is this that Dirk tells me, Elizabeth—he told the same story to his uncle. Why would you do such a dreadful thing—to risk their lives...' She choked back a sob. 'Thank heaven Alexander was here, on the point of leaving for Utrecht hospital to perform an urgent operation, and now thanks to you, the patient may be dead.'

The professor had crossed to where Beth was standing. He took her cold hands in his and said gently: 'Beth, will you not tell us what happened? You had some reason...'

Why, she wondered wearily, were they so sure that it was her fault, and why had Alexander been so cruelly angry with her? She pulled her hands away and said in a wooden little voice: 'Dirk told you—I've nothing to add to that. I'm very sorry about your patient. I hope you'll still be in time.'

She didn't look at either of them but went upstairs to her room, feeling suddenly exhausted.

It seemed hours later when Mevrouw Thorbecke knocked and came in. She said at once: 'Alexander left at once to go to Utrecht, but he wants to talk to you. He will be back tomorrow evening. Beth, it is a great disappointment to me that this has happened. The children...you must understand...I almost died of anxiety. You have been so good with them too.'

She paused and Beth said in a matter-of-fact voice: 'You would like me to leave, wouldn't you? I'll pack my things.'

'But you must stay to see Alexander.' Mevrouw Thorbecke gave her a sharp glance. 'I thought—you and he...he will wish to see you.'

'I can't think of any reason why he should want to see me,' said Beth steadily. 'He knows what happened, Dirk told him.' If there was bitterness in her voice, her companion didn't notice it.

'Then you will go in the morning? You wish to fly, or will you go by boat? You have money enough?'

'Yes, thank you, and I'll go by boat, there's one at

midday from the Hoek, isn't there?' Beth spoke at random, not caring how she went.

Mevrouw Thorbecke went to the door. 'Very well, I will arrange for the car to take you to Rotterdam. You will be able to manage from there?'

'Yes, thank you.' They were both being so polite, thought Beth wildly. 'May I say goodbye to the children? I'll tell them I've been recalled to hospital.'

Mevrouw Thorbecke nodded. 'I will see that some supper is sent up,' she said as she went.

Beth had been in bed for hours when she remembered that neither of them had thought any more about her supper.

The children were all in the schoolroom when Beth went along the next morning to say good-bye, and obviously no one had told them that she was going; they clamoured to know why she hadn't had her breakfast with them, which gave her a good opportunity to tell them that she was leaving. She shook them by the hand in turn, explaining exactly why the hospital wanted her back, and Marineka and Alberdina complicated matters by crying bitterly at her news. Even Hubert snivelled a little, so that she was forced to be so bright and cheerful herself that she felt that her face would crack with the effort of keeping a smile on it, but she managed, even when she said good-bye to Dirk, standing a little apart from the others.

She was surprised when he clung to her hand.

'You're being sent away?' he asked low-voiced. 'It's because of yesterday, isn't it? I told them…I am a coward, for I did not speak the truth, Beth. I remembered what my uncle said to me that day, when we climbed the cliff, and I did not dare to tell.'

'What did he say, dear?' asked Beth gently.

'If I am a good boy, then when my father returns I am to go with my mother to meet him; there is to be a reception and much splendour, but my uncle said that if I did anything foolish again, I would not go.'

He raised miserable eyes to hers. Beth's stiff little smile became warm and kind. 'Don't worry, Dirk, it doesn't matter, nothing matters any more.' She sighed. 'Only promise me that you'll not do anything so foolish again, not when your brother and sisters are with you. You're the eldest son and when your father's away you have to take care of them and your mother. You'll be able to have all the adventure you want when you're grown up.'

He was staring at her. 'You didn't sneak on me to Uncle Alexander that day, did you? I thought you did because he knew all about it—how did he know that I had been rude?—and so I said that I wouldn't like you any more and that I would pay you out. Oh, Beth…'

Her smile widened. 'No, I didn't sneak, Dirk, and I expect your uncle guessed that bit about you being rude—he's been a boy too, you know. It's nice that we part friends, though.'

They shook hands again and with a final wave to them all she slipped out of the room. She could hear the little girls' wails as she hurried down to the hall, where Mevrouw Thorbecke was waiting, but Beth paused only as long as was polite; her heart was frozen inside her and she couldn't think; she had had her copybook blotted, even though she hadn't done it herself, and there was nothing left to do but tear out the page.

The boat was full of cheerful holidaymakers and it seemed a long time before it docked at Harwich, but at least she had had the time to make some plans; she would go back to St Elmer's, of course, back to the Recovery Room and the busy rushing life between her work and the shabby little flat, but she knew that she wouldn't be able to stay there. William would be ready to move on soon, she would give up the flat when he did and go somewhere right away—Canada or New Zealand—the other side of the world; she couldn't get further away from Alexander than that.

She went through Customs hardly knowing that she had done so and boarded the train, and because she hadn't slept the night before, she slept at once, and didn't wake until the train crawled between the blackened brick-lined approach to Liverpool Street. She tidied herself perfunctorily, not caring in the least how she looked, her violet eyes enormous in her pinched white face, her hair straggling from its confining pins. She lugged her case on to the platform and stood, aimless, while the passengers pushed and jostled past her. She noticed none of them; she was thinking about Alexander again.

Professor van Zeust rounded off his lecture with his usual brilliance, nodded briefly to his audience and left the lecture hall. It was not yet twelve o'clock, but he had already done a teaching round, been to see the patient he had operated upon the previous evening and briefed his housemen, and now, after lunch, there would be a heavy outpatients clinic. But outside the lecture hall he stopped, asked his astonished registrar if he would be good enough to take his afternoon's work for him, and made for the entrance. He had driven the Aston Martin that morning; he thanked heaven for that now as he got into the car and began the drive to Willemstad. He drove at speed; the emergency case had forced him to leave without seeing Beth the evening before, but nothing was going to stop him from seeing her now.

It was Dirk who saw him when he reached his house and came leaping downstairs two at a time to meet him.

'Hullo,' said the professor. 'You'll break a leg if you come downstairs at that rate,' and then at the sight of his nephew's face: 'What's wrong, boy?'

Dirk drew a deep breath. 'Mother said she couldn't telephone you because you would be busy and couldn't be interrupted, but she must have, because you're here.'

His uncle eyed him thoughtfully. 'Your mother didn't telephone me, Dirk. I've come to see Beth.'

The boy gulped, holding back the tears in his eyes because his father and his well-loved uncle had told him that boys of ten didn't cry. 'It's about Beth, Uncle Alexander. She's—she's gone, and it's my fault.'

He looked apprehensively at the tall man before him and was reassured by his calm. 'Gone, has she? In that case let's go somewhere quiet and you shall tell me all about it.'

Dirk hung back. 'You'll be angry.'

'Probably, but you'll take it like a man, I fancy, and you'll feel better once it's off your chest.'

They crossed the hall together, the very large man and the small boy, and went into the study, a room seldom entered by anyone when the master of the house was absent. The professor seated himself on the edge of the desk between the windows and said comfortably: 'When you're ready, boy,' and smiled. He looked so placid that Dirk took heart.

'I took the *boeier*,' he began. 'I wanted to make Beth frightened—I made the others go with me, and when she found us and tried to stop me I wouldn't, so she came too. We had already cast off and she had to swim in all her clothes.' He paused to look at his uncle who was studying his shoes, his face hidden, but 'Go on,' he was encouraged with no sign of anger.

'What happened next?' the professor added casually. 'Can Beth swim?'

'Only just—she's a girl, you see—she flounders.' He went on in a shamed little voice: 'We laughed at her and she must have been frightened.'

His uncle didn't reply, and something about his silence made Dirk hurry on. 'I never meant to go so far, but the wind caught us and we couldn't turn back; we did try, but we almost capsized. We got frightened then, and Beth was scared too, but she didn't cry.'

'But you managed to steer some sort of course. Let us see, Bruinesse wasn't too far, was it, or couldn't you beach the boat?'

'We tried, ever so many times, but we couldn't get the engine to do anything, and Beth doesn't know anything about sailing, so it was a bit difficult. I did remember about Bruinesse, but the wind was too strong, and besides, we couldn't see the land.'

'So?'

'So I steered and Beth found a chart of the engine and she got it to go. We were almost at Brouwershaven by then, so we—that is, Beth, sailed into the harbour; she did something to the engine and it stopped and she got the sails down too, but we did bump one or two yachts. Will Papa be very angry?'

'Furious, I daresay, but I suggest that we don't tell him until he is home again—after his arrival at the airport.'

Nephew and uncle exchanged glances. 'And now

I want to know why you allowed Beth to take the blame, Dirk.'

The boy nodded, sucking in his breath. 'Yes, Uncle. You see, I was afraid you would remember what you said would happen if I did anything silly again, like climbing that cliff, and—and I thought that Beth had sneaked on me and told you I'd been disobedient and rude...'

The professor inspected his nails. 'She didn't sneak; she asked me not to punish you. It was a pretty low-down thing to do, wasn't it, Dirk?'

'Yes—I'm sorry; I like her very much. When she came to say good-bye she was nice. I wanted to tell someone then, but she said I wasn't to—she said it didn't matter—no, what she said was "Nothing matters any more", but when she'd gone I knew I'd have to tell you and I asked Mama to telephone you... Are you very angry, Uncle Alexander? How will you punish me?'

The professor had got to his feet and put a hand on the boy's shoulder. 'I'm not going to punish you, boy,' he said quietly. 'You've had enough already, I fancy. Your father must know, of course—later, as I said. Just promise me that you won't risk anyone else's life again, nor your own unless the circumstances call for it. Word of a Dutchman.'

They shook hands solemnly and the professor said: 'It takes pluck to own up. I'm glad you did.' He walked to the door. 'Now I must be off.'

'Where to, Uncle?'

'Why, England, of course, to find Beth.'

His nephew smiled shakily. 'Oh, super!'

'Let us hope so,' agreed the professor. 'Any idea how she went?'

'I asked Mother. From the Hoek by the midday boat.'

His uncle grinned suddenly. 'That means about eight o'clock at Liverpool Street. If I cut a few corners and go from Calais with the Hovercraft—tell your mother where I've gone, and not a word about our little talk, we'll deal with that later. *Tot ziens.*'

The crowd had thinned now; people had found family or friends, and those who had none had formed an orderly queue for the taxis. Beth picked up her case and looked around her; she supposed that she would have to go somewhere. St Elmer's; but wouldn't it look a bit strange turning up unheralded at half past eight in the evening? She would go to the flat and hope that William wouldn't be there. She started walking slowly along the platform and looked up to see the professor walking very fast towards her. Her first thought was that fate had played a cruel trick on her. He often came to London; it would have to be this very day and time, and in all the city's vastness, they had to meet here. She turned round and hurried, hampered dreadfully by the case, in the opposite direction. No use, of course. She was caught, the case taken from her and dumped on the platform, and she was twirled round, to be wrapped tenderly in Alexander's arms and kissed.

It was like having every happiness there was in the world, rolled into one and handed to her on a plate. All the same, after an endless moment, she made herself say 'No,' in a half-hearted way.

'Yes,' said the professor, 'my darling girl, yes. People kiss on railway stations, hadn't you noticed?' He kissed her again, and Beth, who could think of nothing to say, kissed him back and then coming a little to her senses, said fiercely: 'You didn't even ask me! I couldn't stay another minute...'

'My poor little love! I was out of my mind with worry, imagining you drowned—why didn't you explain?'

The unfairness of this remark caused her to pull away from him, a useless thing to do, for he merely held her more tightly. 'Explain? How could I explain when you were quite ready to believe that I'd taken the boat—the last thing I'd do; I don't know one end from another, and I've never been so terrified.' She looked up at him. 'Why are you laughing?' Her violet eyes flashed with temper and then filled with tears. 'Oh, Alexander, you were so angry...'

'My little love, when the police telephoned and I knew you were safe I wanted to kiss you and choke you and hug you—you see, you had given me the fright of my life.'

He kissed her once more, and the porter who had come to a halt beside them waited patiently until he had done before asking: 'Take your bag, sir?'

The professor lifted his head and blinked at the man. 'There's a car parked behind the taxi rank, an Aston Martin—put the case on the pavement beside it, will you?' He took an arm from Beth and felt in a pocket and handed the man some coins. As the man went away Beth said: 'Someone will take it, you know.'

'We'll buy whatever you need tomorrow.'

She stared up at him. 'But what about tonight?'

He went on speaking as though he hadn't heard her. 'Caundle Bubb—we can be there in three hours—no, four. We'll have a meal on the way and I must telephone the hospital and get someone to take over for a day or two.'

'Why?' asked Beth in an excited little voice.

'I thought we might get married…'

'I don't remember being asked,' she told him tartly.

'Dear heart, I'm asking you now. It did cross my mind to do so when we first met, but we hardly knew each other, did we?'

She smiled up at him and he said softly: 'I love you, little Beth, there's no one in the world I want but you—will you come with me?'

Her head was stuffed full with questions, but they could wait. She lifted her face to be kissed and said in a voice which shook a little with excitement and happiness: 'Yes, Alexander darling, I'll come with you.'

Welcome to cowboy country...

Turn the page for a sneak preview of
TEXAS BABY
by
Kathleen O'Brien
An exciting new title from Harlequin Superromance
for everyone who loves stories about the West.

Harlequin Superromance—
Where life and love weave together in emotional and
unforgettable ways.

CHAPTER ONE

CHASE TRANSFERRED his gaze to the road and identified a foreign spot on the horizon. A car. Almost half a mile away, where the straight, tree-lined drive met the public road. He could tell it was coming too fast, but judging the speed of a vehicle moving straight toward you was tricky.

It wasn't until it was about two hundred yards away that he realized the driver must be drunk...or crazy. Or both.

The guy was going maybe sixty. On a private drive, out here in ranch country, where kids or horses or tractors or stupid chickens might come darting out any minute, that was criminal. Chase straightened from his comfortable slouch and waved his hands.

"Slow down, you fool," he called out. He took the porch steps quickly and began walking fast down the driveway.

The car veered oddly, from one lane to another,

then up onto the slight rise of the thick green spring grass. It just barely missed the fence.

"Slow down, damn it!"

He couldn't see the driver, and he didn't recognize this automobile. It was small and old, and couldn't have cost much even when it was new. It was probably white, but now it needed either a wash or a new paint job or both.

"Damn it, what's wrong with you?"

At the last minute, he had to jump away, because the idiot behind the wheel clearly wasn't going to turn to avoid a collision. He couldn't believe it. The car kept coming, finally slowing a little, but it was too late.

Still going about thirty miles an hour, it slammed into the large, white-brick pillar that marked the front boundaries of the house. The pillar wasn't going to give an inch, so the car had to. The front end folded up like a paper fan.

It seemed to take forever for the car to settle, as if the trauma happened in slow motion, reverberating from the front to the back of the car in ripples of destruction. The front windshield suddenly seemed to ice over with lethal bits of glassy frost. Then the side windows exploded.

The front driver's door wrenched open, as if the car wanted to expel its contents. Metal buckled hideously. Small pieces, like hubcaps and mirrors, skipped and ricocheted insanely across the oyster-shell driveway.

Finally, everything was still. Into the silence, a plume of steam shot up like a geyser, smelling of rust and heat. Its snake-like hiss almost smothered the low, agonized moan of the driver.

Chase's anger had disappeared. He didn't feel anything but a dull sense of disbelief. Things like this didn't happen in real life. Not in his life. Maybe the sun had actually put him to sleep....

But he was already kneeling beside the car. The driver was a woman. The frosty glass-ice of the windshield was dotted with small flecks of blood. She must have hit it with her head, because just below her hairline a red liquid was seeping out. He touched it. He tried to wipe it away before it reached her eyebrow, though, of course that made no sense at all. Her eyes were shut.

Was she conscious? Did he dare move her? Her dress was covered in glass, and the metal of the car was sticking out lethally in all the wrong places.

Then he remembered, with an intense relief, that every good medical man in the county was here, just behind the house, drinking his champagne. He found his phone and paged Trent.

The woman moaned again.

Alive, then. Thank God for that.

He saw Trent coming toward him, starting out at a lope, but quickly switching to a full run.

"Get Dr. Marchant," Chase called. "Don't bother with 911."

Trent didn't take long to assess the situation. A

fraction of a second, and he began pulling out his cell phone and running toward the house.

The yelling seemed to have roused the woman. She opened her eyes. They were blue and clouded with pain and confusion.

"Chase," she said.

His breath stalled. His head pulled back. "What?"

Her only answer was another moan, and he wondered if he had imagined the word. He reached around her and put his arm behind her shoulders. She was tiny. Probably petite by nature, but surely way too thin. He could feel her shoulder blades pushing against her skin, as fragile as the wishbone in a turkey.

She seemed to have passed out, so he put his other arm under her knees and lifted her out. He tried to avoid the jagged metal, but her skirt caught on a piece and the tearing sound seemed to wake her again.

"No," she said. "Please."

"I'm just trying to help," he said. "It's going to be all right."

She seemed profoundly distressed. She wriggled in his arms, and she was so weak, like a broken bird. It made him feel too big and brutish. And intrusive. As if touching her this way, his bare hands against the warm skin behind her knees, were somehow a transgression.

He wished he could be more delicate. But he smelled gasoline, and he knew it wasn't safe to leave her here.

Finally he heard the sound of voices, as guests

began to run around the side of the house, alerted by Trent. Dr. Marchant was at the front, racing toward them as if he were forty instead of seventy. Susannah was right behind him, her green dress floating around her trim legs.

"Please," the woman in his arms murmured again. She looked at him, the expression in her blue eyes lost and bewildered. He wondered if she might be on drugs. Hitting her head on the windshield might account for this unfocused, glazed look, but it couldn't explain the crazy driving.

"Please, put me down. Susannah... The wedding..."

Chase's arms tightened instinctively, and he froze in his tracks. She whimpered, and he realized he might be hurting her. "Say that again?"

"The wedding. I have to stop it."

* * * * *

Be sure to look for TEXAS BABY,
available September 11, 2007,
as well as other fantastic Superromance titles
available in September.

HARLEQUIN *Super Romance*

Welcome to Cowboy Country...

TEXAS BABY

by *Kathleen O'Brien*

#1441

Chase Clayton doesn't know what to think.
A beautiful stranger has just crashed his
engagement party, demanding that he not
marry because she's pregnant with his baby.
But the kicker is—he's never seen her before.

Look for TEXAS BABY and other fantastic
Superromance titles on sale September 2007.

Available wherever books are sold.

HARLEQUIN *Super Romance*

Where life and love weave together
in emotional and unforgettable ways.

HARLEQUIN *Presents*

Always passionate, always proud.

**The richest royal family in the world—
a family united by blood and passion,
torn apart by deceit and desire.**

By royal decree, Harlequin Presents is delighted to bring
you The Royal House of Niroli. Step into the glamorous,
enticing world of the Nirolian Royal Family. As the king
ails he must find an heir. Each month an exciting new
installment follows the epic search for the true Nirolian
king. Eight heirs, eight romances, eight fantastic stories!

Coming in September:

BOUGHT BY THE BILLIONAIRE PRINCE
by Carol Marinelli

Luca Fierezza is ruthless, a rogue and a rebel....
Megan Donavan's stunned when she's thrown into
jail and her unlikely rescuer is her new boss, Luca!
But now she's also entirely at his mercy...in his bed!

**Be sure not to miss any of the passion!
Coming in October:**

THE TYCOON'S PRINCESS BRIDE
by Natasha Oakley

www.eHarlequin.com

HP12659

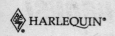

HARLEQUIN®

EVERLASTING LOVE™

Every great love has a story to tell™

Third time's a charm.

Texas summers. Charlie Morrison.
Jasmine Boudreaux has always connected
the two. Her relationship with Charlie
begins and ends in high school. Twenty
years later it begins again—and ends again.
Now fate has stepped in one more time—
will Jazzy and Charlie finally give in to
the love they've shared all this time?

Look for

Summer After Summer
by
Ann DeFee

**Available September
wherever books are sold.**

www.eHarlequin.com   HESAS0907

REQUEST YOUR FREE BOOKS!
2 FREE NOVELS PLUS 2
FREE GIFTS!

HARLEQUIN ROMANCE®

From the Heart, For the Heart

YES! Please send me 2 FREE Harlequin Romance® novels and my 2 FREE gifts. After receiving them, if I don't wish to receive any more books, I can return the shipping statement marked "cancel." If I don't cancel, I will receive 4 brand-new novels every month and be billed just $3.57 per book in the U.S., or $4.05 per book in Canada, plus 25¢ shipping and handling per book and applicable taxes, if any*. That's a savings of over 15% off the cover price! I understand that accepting the 2 free books and gifts places me under no obligation to buy anything. I can always return a shipment and cancel at any time. Even if I never buy another book from Harlequin, the two free books and gifts are mine to keep forever.

114 HDN EEV7 314 HDN EEWK

Name	(PLEASE PRINT)	
Address		Apt.
City	State/Prov.	Zip/Postal Code

Signature (if under 18, a parent or guardian must sign)

Mail to the **Harlequin Reader Service®**:
IN U.S.A.: P.O. Box 1867, Buffalo, NY 14240-1867
IN CANADA: P.O. Box 609, Fort Erie, Ontario L2A 5X3

Not valid to current Harlequin Romance subscribers.

Want to try two free books from another line?
Call 1-800-873-8635 or visit www.morefreebooks.com.

* Terms and prices subject to change without notice. NY residents add applicable sales tax. Canadian residents will be charged applicable provincial taxes and GST. This offer is limited to one order per household. All orders subject to approval. Credit or debit balances in a customer's account(s) may be offset by any other outstanding balance owed by or to the customer. Please allow 4 to 6 weeks for delivery.

Your Privacy: Harlequin is committed to protecting your privacy. Our Privacy Policy is available online at www.eHarlequin.com or upon request from the Reader Service. From time to time we make our lists of customers available to reputable firms who may have a product or service of interest to you. If you would prefer we not share your name and address, please check here. ☐

HR07